PRAISE FOR

'In this intricate and subtle wonder (

writer of breathtaking insight and empathy. Like a ray......

Australian suburbs, she chronicles the lives of these ordinary characters with love,

humour and sharp precision. At once restrained and honest, unsentimental and

deeply moving, *Barking Dogs* is indeed something both special and rare.'

Emily Bitto

'This subtle book has a spare, light surface, and startlingly memorable depths. The

threads that bind it together are either stark and architectural, or all but invisible.

Rebekah Clarkson's work is one of compassion without sentiment; great art

without flamboyance or ego. An extraordinary first work of fiction.'

Eva Hornung

'Rebekah Clarkson takes us to a place of intimacy and isolation, community and

cruelty that we recognise, with pleasure and alarm, as the way we live now.'

Nicholas Jose

'A distinctly Australian allegory of urban sprawl, McMansions and the plight

of the aspirational classes mortgaged to the hilt ... Fans of short fiction with

a strong Australian flavour will appreciate Clarkson's satisfying use of both

the novel and short-story forms, and her ability to sketch intimately relatable

characters with humour and generosity, silhouetted against a devastating

panorama of contemporary Australia.'

Books+Publishing

Neil Gaiman — truth is not what happens but what it tells us about who we are.

Fiction is the lie that tells the truth.

"The novel is a pack of lies hounding the truth."
                              Carlos Fuentes.

"All good novelists have bad memories"
   Graeme Green.

ROB. — what you remember comes out as journalism. What you forget goes into the compost of the imagination.

_____

                              Hillman
                              Hashwell

         Mary + Ron

         Rich + Lorraine Hashwell!
                Archie

_____

      Sandra Cisneros
   Your own neighbourhood as home
   unique as worthy of writing about.
   what is 'exotic'?

James Joyce Dubliners —
the way connection + disconnection
mimics the way a real life community
works.

town – 175 yrs.
– settled in 1844
– The truest lies I can tell.
Questions of land ownership + belonging are an ever present tension or under w/land

Rebekah Clarkson's award-winning fiction has been published widely, most recently in *Best Australian Stories*, *Australian Book Review* and *Something Special, Something Rare: Outstanding Short Stories by Australian Women* (Black Inc.). Her stories have been recognised in major awards in Australia and overseas, including the *ABR* Elizabeth Jolley Short Story Prize and *Glimmer Train*'s Fiction Open. She has a BA in Aboriginal Studies and a PhD in Creative Writing from the University of Adelaide, where she also teaches. She has taught Fiction Writing at the University of Texas in Austin.

Graham + Jenny Barlow
Sophie + Liam

4 stories: Malcolm + Theresa Whelan
Martin

Edna + Andrea (Greg)
(Brian)

Nathan Hearle + Kelly
Braydon + Ella

Donna + Roger
Amelia

Socrates:
"The unexamined life isn't worth living."
(Reading is one way we can examine our lives. ?)]

Siri Hustvedt:
"Writing fiction is like remembering what never happened."

Flannery O'Connor + Raymond Carver
- doesn't sympathise = their characters or seek to justify themselves through their characters.
- you don't pander but you can have compassion.

M + B.
Homogenous – culturally + sexually
2011 census – 40% large
other than
English.

BARKING DOGS

Curious about my town –
not facts + stats but for
its psyche – its subterranean
"truths"

the novel is a pack of
lies hounding the
truth.

REBEKAH CLARKSON

– Could I capture
something that is unique
about M + B?
– Could I put an imagined
representation –
a translation –
of M + B on
the literary
map?

⟹ Barking Dog.

AFFIRM press

AFFIRM press

Published by Affirm Press in 2017
28 Thistlethwaite Street, South Melbourne, VIC 3205.
www.affirmpress.com.au

National Library of Australia Cataloguing-in-Publication entry available
for this title.
Title: Barking Dogs / Rebekah Clarkson, author.
ISBN: 9781925475494 (paperback)

Cover design by Karen Wallis, Taloula Press
Front cover image: Nick Bowers/Getty Images
Author photo: David Washington
Typeset in 12/16 Garamond Premier Pro by J&M Typesetting
Proudly printed in Australia by Griffin Press

MIX
Paper from
responsible sources
FSC **FSC® C009448**
www.fsc.org

The paper this book is printed on is certified against the Forest Stewardship
Council® Standards. Griffin Press holds FSC chain of custody certification SGS-
COC-005088. FSC promotes environmentally responsible, socially beneficial
and economically viable management of the world's forests.

*This is a work of fiction. Names, characters, businesses, places, events and
incidents are either the products of the author's imagination or used in a
fictitious manner. No identification with actual persons is intended or should
be inferred.*

4 do
13 stories.

For Amos

Here We Lie	1 – 12
Something S, Something R	13 – 33 †
World Peace	35 – 46 †
Raising Boys	47 – 63 †
Hold Me Close	64 – 82
The 4th Dimension	83 – 95
The 5 Truths of Manhood	96 – 112
Dancing on Jaw Bones	113 – 140 †
May Twentieth	141 · 148
The Honesty Window	149 – 172
What I Wished	173 – 188
Jasper	190 – 220
If It Wasn't This	221 – 230

HERE WE LIE

We found the body of Lorelie Hastwell on the floor of the Hastwell family dining room. We knew she was dead. We knew it as soon as the back door was down. At first we gulped it, as if death was cold beer, but then we gagged and Troy Campbell retched. We pulled our shirts up over our mouths and noses as we made our way in. Rotting food on the kitchen table and in the sink. Dishes everywhere. Shit all over the floor; shit we didn't expect: piles of paper, crumpled paper, old rags, dried weeds, dead flowers. We had to step on it to get down the hallway. Drawings all over the walls: the actual walls. Pencil, texta, pen, paint and something else, something like dried blood. But the drawings were good, we could see that. Drawings of plants; plants we knew. Fennel and rye grass, wheat, caltrop, Salvation Jane. There were flowers too. Roses. All over the walls. We remembered then: Lorelie always said she was going to be an artist. Years ago, she said that.

We all had the same question: when was the last time

anyone had been in this house? She'd locked it up when we did the backyard blitz. We had to use the dunny at the pub because we couldn't get in. Not even our wives had been here. Our wives, who thought they knew everything there was to know. It dawned on us – no one had been in this house since her parents died. No one had seen what we were seeing.

Lorelie's eyes were closed but her mouth was open. She seemed on the verge of saying something. Her frozen expression looked like she'd walked into the room and forgotten why she did. Lorelie was always like that: not here, not there. By her side was a bottle from Chemmart labelled *Temazepam*. Later, we showed that bottle to the police. A simple and obvious piece of evidence. But there were other things too, things we didn't show.

There were more drawings, not of plants or flowers. Lorelie had placed them around the space where she planned to lie. Drawings of faces and bodies, twisted and warped. We knew they were good drawings. There were paintings too. Canvases. We didn't need to count five; we could see them. Four were propped against each leg of the mahogany dining table, and the fifth – the paint still wet, we could smell the oils – lay next to Lorelie's head. We took a sharp breath when we saw them, our shirts sucked into the hollows of our mouths. There were five of us. Someone said, 'Jesus.' No one said anything more.

By unspoken agreement, and there were a few of these – in between calling the police and the undertaker (we went with Crouch and Sons) and them both arriving – we stacked the five canvases and a pile of the sketches in another room, right out of the way. We stacked them under Rich and Lorraine's old bed. We moved quickly. We moved quietly. All we could hear was our own muffled breathing and our boots as they scuffed across that old Hastwell carpet. Memories were tumbling. Stuff we'd forgotten about. And we knew we were removing objects from the scene of a dubious death, but we let that go.

We're good men. Locals. Longest-serving members of the Mount Barker Summit Club. There are a few newbies in the club – the tree changers – but we're the locals. Some of our families go back five generations. We've known Lorelie since she was a girl, since we were boys. We've worked for Rich Hastwell at the fodder shop or the car dealership or R & L Fencing, or all three. Bursar of one of the local schools, tax accountant, car dealer and two in real estate: we're a mixed bunch.

We're busy men: president, deputy president, secretary of the football club. We've got our jobs, our sport, our families, and we're proud of what we've done around here. Our members built the spectator benches at the Lang Street tennis courts. We planted five hundred trees in the wetlands, landscaped the bowling club, organised relief packs for the bushfire victims in Victoria. We support the boys who wanna have a crack at their footy down in the city, raising scholarships for talented young players like John Risby's lad. We've fundraised a dozen local projects over the years. Helped out less fortunate members in our community.

Less fortunate. This is where it started with Lorelie, with the backyard blitz. None of us had spoken to her in years. Hadn't had anything to do with her. We'd planted the rose bush and installed the plaque at the Council chambers – a tribute to Rich and Lorraine Hastwell for their years of contribution, not just in business and employment in this town, but also in the Baptist church, the school ... Lorraine's work with the choir. Rich Hastwell *founded* the Summit Club – we were just kids then. It was our wives who got all obsessed about Lorelie again.

The backyard blitz was their idea. 'It will be just what she needs,' they said. We heard this a lot, this phrase 'just what she needs'. It was also our wives' idea to send Lorelie away for the weekend so we could surprise her at the end. 'Like on TV,' they said. Profits from the February and March sausage sizzles paid for two nights at Wirrina Cove Resort. It appealed to their female sense of drama. The girls pictured Lorelie roaming the golf course. They pictured blindfolding her on the Sunday night. They said things like: 'She'll probably cry!' and 'She'll be overwhelmed, just overwhelmed!' None of us five wanted to see Lorelie blindfolded.

The Hastwell property had become an eyesore in the middle of town. Being a Hastwell doesn't make any difference to a weed. It was hard work hacking out all that caltrop, Salvation Jane, sow thistle, rye grass as tall as any one of us. We joked that caltrop doesn't know history or share prices or bank balances. Caltrop couldn't care less that this was Hastwell property. We laughed about that as we pulled it all out.

~

Everybody thinks they know this story. They tell it on the main street, in the school canteen, the clubrooms, the pub. Our wives tell it over and over into the phone.

They start with the wealthiest, oldest family in town. They embellish the freakish truck accident on the expressway – one minute the Hastwells own the town, the next they're lying in their graves, every bone broken, ashes literally to ashes, dust to dust, decomposed before they've even made it close to those mahogany, satin-lined coffins. Then the stock market crash, the dying businesses: cars, fodder, fencing respectively. Then the image of Lorelie rumbling around alone in the big old house, only her own Mercedes in the driveway now, *Lorelie* printed on the numberplate like it was on each of her coloured pencils in primary school.

This is how everybody tells the story. Then they flag the robbery; probably just kids, but still. The backyard blitz comes next (indicative of the true rallying nature of this community). But as the story goes, the blitz was too much and it wasn't enough. These are the words that everybody uses when they tell this story: too much and not enough. And they are still telling it. 'The backyard thing the boys did,' we heard Noelene Clark say to Megan Munro at the funeral, 'it just seemed to throw her.' Everybody knows about the Temazepam.

She'd been dead three days, the coroner told us. No one, not ever, when they tell this story, stops to consider the stench. There's no mention of it in the gospels either, nothing we can remember from Sunday school; we've left all that behind. 'Asleep, coma, dead,' they say, and, 'She felt no pain.' Those in the know finish with one last detail: the members of the Summit Club found her, the same men who'd done the backyard blitz. They used an angle grinder on the back security door of that big old house, and they were the ones who called for the police and Crouch.

That was us: we were the ones. But nobody knows about the rest. Nobody knows about the other stuff. The stuff we try not to remember when we lie awake at night.

~

Our wives were right. She cried that day, the day of the blitz. But they weren't tears of joy. There was even talk that we should unblitz the blitz – take it all apart, dig it all out: the grevilleas, the row of screening pittosporums, the fruit trees; Meyer lemon, blood orange and Satsuma plum; the rosemary and lavender hedges; the 'reflection bench' under the elm and even – especially, as it turned out – the outdoor entertaining area.

We'd been quietly proud of the outdoor entertaining area. It was the grand finale of our entire effort. We'd thought it out carefully, cemented and then bolted the wooden table and the benches deep down into that rich dirt. We'd thought cementing it in would give Lorelie a sense of security, a sense of permanence. No one said this, no one mentioned the security factor and why we bolted it all down; it was a natural thing, a given, and we all held the idea of it like a non-negotiable fact, another mathematical reality as we mapped it out, drew it up, collected our materials and dug it through, with a little bit of help from Bob Lang's Dingo digger. No one could steal the table and the benches in the night. No one could move them or even change their location in the backyard. We'd thought this was a good thing. We'd thought we were doing Lorelie a favour.

We'd thought it might be enough. We didn't think of the word 'redemption', but we knew it and we felt it; we felt that word in our marrow.

Everybody knew about the Christmas Eve robbery. It wasn't headline news, just in the police section of the *Courier*. Lorelie's old bicycle and a microwave from the back porch. Nothing irreplaceable. Our wives all said the same thing: that we wouldn't understand. 'It's not about what's taken. It's not about *things*,' they said, as if we were missing words and concepts from the English language. 'It's the violation of privacy. Of *Lorelie's* privacy.'

'*Poor Lorelie*,' was what they said.

Crime is growing in this town at the rate of weeds, and we haven't seen the worst of it. Newer estates are cropping up now like mushroom farms – 300 square metres apiece; you could reach over the fence and open your neighbour's toilet window, gifting him with fresh air. More strangers than familiar faces around here now. Once, you knew everybody and everything. All as familiar as the Hastwell place, right down to the turret-like stone fixtures, crumbling now, like untended gravestones on every corner of the old house.

Lorelie walked through her back gate that Sunday afternoon, one of our wives on either side, resolute on clutching each of Lorelie's arms. We thanked God they let go of the blindfolding idea. It was obvious the weekend at Wirrina hadn't reached the heights of any group vision. Dishevelled and slightly unsteady, Lorelie looked more as though she were being escorted home after a stay in hospital. She looked old, and although we knew she wasn't any older than us, we hadn't seen her for a while and a lot of water had passed under the bridge.

At first, she just stood there inside the gate. We couldn't tell by the wobbling on her face whether it was unbridled joy, or unbridled something else. Suddenly, then, she untangled her arms and started running – *loping*, is more accurate – around the perimeter of the new garden. We were still unsure, but we were worried. There was something of an injured wild animal about her, and it was discomfiting for everyone watching. Most of us were still there, and three or four of the girls. Troy Campbell had left by then, and John Risby with his youngest lad.

Lorelie stopped still when she saw our entertaining area. Her shoulders dropped forward and her chest slumped. Then she lunged herself toward the table – a row of thick planks we'd salvaged from Bob Lang's property. She grabbed the edges in her hands and fairly threw her whole body weight, not insubstantial, backward and forward. The table didn't budge, naturally; we'd used 5-inch bolts and four bags of cement (donated by Mitre 10). All that shook was Lorelie.

Everyone watching took a few steps backward. That unruly hair was flung across her forehead and back again, as though it had a life of its own, as though it were a creature, furry and brown, that Lorelie was desperate to be rid of.

Nathan Hearle's comment at The Barker afterwards: 'Lorelie,' he'd said, pronouncing 'lie' as 'lee', and it wasn't the first time; another reminder to us that he was a newcomer. Hearle didn't know anything about anyone or anything. 'She was like a madwoman at a heavy metal concert,' he'd said, and chuckled with himself.

We'd nodded but none of us spoke. Someone ordered another round.

'I mean, *jeez* ... she's not much of a looker, is she?' Hearle had lifted up his head and looked around as if he'd finally found the courage to say what had been bothering him since she'd appeared at the back gate. We'd all stared into our schooners and then thrown back our Coopers. Sometimes what you do with your beer says more than you say with your mouth.

Hearle was right. Lorelie Hastwell wasn't a girl you wanted, for *anything* – to fuck or marry. We thought of her as nothing. 'She's really a slut,' the girls told us back then. We all pretend we don't remember. We all pretend. We don't even admit to this, to the pretending. There's been a lot of water under the bridge. So much is different up here now. Not everyone is local. There's talk of a KFC. A McDonald's with a drive-through and extended carpark has replaced R & L Fencing, leaving no trace of the Hastwells or the old apricot tree we used to raid green to beat the birds after school. Instead, a manicured box hedge and a row of standard roses: white, just like all the other roses planted at all the other McDonald's. People don't want farm fencing anymore. They want Colorbond. And a Grand Angus beef burger. We want them too. Everything has changed now. What happened back then is like a messed-up roll of film that didn't develop in the dark room. Even our memories are washed out and blurry. Everything's digital now, anyway. You have to move on.

There was a chant in primary school: 'If you step on the cracks, you love Lorrie Hastwell.' It was like a reflex, despising Lorelie: it was a given, it was the way the world was. Things were simpler back then. What you loved, what you hated, what you wanted and what you didn't. It was the same for all of us. Disdain for Lorelie was like disdain for VB or the VFL; it wasn't personal, just the way it was. *If you step on the cracks, you love Lorrie Hastwell.* We'd forgotten about that. Then later, we were in high school. No one did the chant then.

Some of our kids are in high school. Some will be in high school in the next couple of years. A thought like that can stop you in your tracks.

Rich and Lorraine had had high hopes for Lorelie. Never had any other kids. She was meant to be a lawyer or an accountant. Meant to preside over the family empire. She was sent to a private school in the city, boarding at first and then commuting. And then, as quickly as she'd left, she was back with us at the local high. She'd told her parents she wanted to be an artist (we'd forgotten about that). Her mother's shining Mercedes at the pick-up gate. We could see her mother through the windscreen, her hair up in smooth rolls.

~

Lorelie had been saddled with her father's looks. A funny nose with closely knitted eyes. Manageable on an entrepreneur like Rich – possibly even advantageous – but not on his only daughter. All Lorelie collected from her mother was the curl in her hair. Her mother was a looker. We made smutty jokes about her mother. Lorelie, we taunted and teased. That was all. That was all we did. It was a different time, we all know that. People talk in different ways now. But things were different back then. Everything was different.

Now we lie awake at night on our Harvey Norman beds in our cardboard houses, and it's the details that are coming back; all those freckles on her girlish round face, merging around her eyes like birthmarks, the baggy school dress and her scuffed shoes. That look in her eyes. The only reason we used the school shirt to cover her face. It was like she was seeing us in a way we couldn't see ourselves. Well, clearly she was.

We got rid of those paintings, but it was too late. Because they were good. Those faces – our faces – are etched now in our minds. We try not to look at each other too closely these days. We try not to catch each other's eyes.

Lorelie: always teetering precariously between success and failure, hinged and unhinged, alive and non-existent.

~

We were the pallbearers. No one else came forward: it was as simple as that. We thought there was a cousin in the city – Hastwell's Auto Transmission – but they'd moved to Queensland and didn't come down, some bad blood over the wills. No family at the funeral, just us and our wives and kids and anyone else who remembered the Hastwells: had worked in the fodder shop or the car dealership or R & L Fencing, or all three. A good number from the church were there. Some of the old members of the choir sang 'Amazing Grace' and 'Oh Perfect Love'. Bette Midler singing 'Wind Beneath My Wings' was played as we walked out with the coffin, the weight of Lorelie bearing down on our shoulders.

There was a moment in the service when the minister read aloud the quote they'd put on the program; it was printed right under the blurry photo of Lorelie. 'Yesterday is a memory,' he said, 'tomorrow is a mystery and today is a gift.' He paused then and looked directly at us, sitting in the front row because we were the pallbearers, 'which is why it is called the present.' We heard sniffling, someone crying behind us. And then we all felt it, all at once – nothing needed to be said. It wasn't guilt then, or shame, or even sadness. But we all felt it.

Like the stench, sharp and unfamiliar, on that day of discovery – 21 March, it was a Saturday, stinking hot – when we cut through the back door of the Hastwell house. Our wives had said that something was wrong. They could feel it, they said, and we had to go in. We *owed* it to her, they said. These are the words we use when we talk about Lorelie Hastwell. We say that it was the *least* we could do. We say that we at least *owed* her that. But we never say more. We never say more.

Nothing prepares you for the smell of death. Everyone struggles to describe it; and mostly they don't – because words are like pictures, they can be powerful. Words threaten to live beyond olfactory memory and the nerve endings of your own fear. As with death itself, we hurried wordlessly past its odour.

SOMETHING SPECIAL, SOMETHING RARE

It was not the first time Graham and Liam Barlow had sat in matching chairs on the wrong side of a school principal's desk. Graham folded his arms across his chest and cocked his chin toward his son.

'Was it by accident or on purpose, Liam?'

Liam shook his hair from his forehead. He began to open his mouth as the telephone rang shrill on the desk. The principal picked it up and raised an index finger midair.

Graham tried again to remember the principal's name. Using someone's name was a persuasion tool. Graham had learnt that in the government program he'd done years ago: the New Enterprise Incentive Scheme. His enterprise hadn't worked out; landscaping was hopeless with a crook back, but excellence is a state of mind put into action, they say, and that's why Graham had called his new business 'Winners'. The name was just right: relevant, memorable, a good ring to it. Winners would specialise in supplying medals and trophies to sporting clubs. Graham had a pitch ready for the Hahndorf Football Club, once the president returned his calls. He'd put Troy Campbell into his Contacts so as to be ready, and while the principal talked, Graham dragged his thumb across the Bluetooth headset in his jeans' front pocket. He wished he'd left the earpiece switched on and attached. He was a businessman, with work to do and people to see. He wouldn't even be here if Jenny hadn't refused to leave TAFE for the afternoon. She'd missed enough lessons looking after her mum and dealing with all of Sophie's dramas, she said, and Liam's school didn't need them both to go in. Plus, she said, it was embarrassing.

The principal was making professional cooing sounds into the phone and nodding slowly.

Graham pulled his fingers into fists, resting them on top of his thighs, like kids do in the front row of class photos. Supplying the medals and trophies for Hahndorf Football Club alone would set Winners off and running. He tightened his fists till his knuckles turned white. Then there'd be word of mouth. Then you'd get your tennis, basketball, netball, hockey, all the carnivals. Other towns through the hills and the Fleurieu Peninsula would jump onboard. Everyone would know that Winners had the best product and service, that online wasn't easier or cheaper – though making it cheaper *and* profitable really would depend on the bulk orders coming in. That was his biggest hurdle. It wasn't as if he didn't have a business plan.

'That's as stupid as a birth plan,' Jenny said when he showed it to her. 'You haven't factored in bad luck. Or bad timing. Or bad genes.'

The principal hung up the phone and pursed his lips. When he spoke, it was quiet and deliberate, just like the doctor after Jenny had been in labour for twenty hours.

'Well, that was Mrs Wheeler from the emergency department. Martin has concussion. And he's been given stitches across his left eyebrow.'

The principal paused, but Graham knew what was coming next. The kid could have gone blind. It was always about someone nearly going blind.

'You know, Liam, if your lightsaber had been a couple of centimetres lower, just a fraction lower ...' The principal dropped his chin, leant over the desk.

'Accident?' Liam looked up and turned to Graham, who nodded at his son's answer to the all-important question.

The principal stretched back in his chair and put his hands behind his head. 'How do you think you'd be feeling now, Liam, if Martin was blind in his left eye?'

Liam's mouth flinched to one side. 'Not good?'

'No, that's right. I don't imagine you'd be feeling very good, would you?'

Graham wasn't feeling very good. He visualised his shop locked up again, the hopeful, hand-printed *Back in 5 Minutes* sign stuck on the door with Blu-Tack. He was going to have to close for half a day again tomorrow, in order to drive Jenny down to her mum's in Modbury North. Jenny was refusing to drive on the freeway. 'You're not going to die from driving on the freeway,' Graham had told her, over and over. 'It's not the freeway per se,' she told him, 'it's the trucks.' She said she had a panic attack whenever she saw one coming up in her rear-vision mirror. She said she froze, and when they passed her whole car shivered, and the first time it happened she had tears in her eyes and her life flashed before her like people say it does when you have a near-death experience. She wouldn't drive on the freeway, she said, because a man couldn't raise a girl without a woman around. This was so illogical, so off the point, that Graham hardly knew what to say back. And it miffed him; it wasn't as if Jenny had an all-star relationship with their daughter. Apparently, his was worse.

'Liam, what do you think you could do, to make this right with Martin?' the principal asked.

Graham wondered if he needed to spell it out to the principal himself; the kids were only mucking about, it could have been Liam's eyebrow with stitches, and it wasn't a lightsaber, it was just a stupid stick. There seemed to be a fine line when you were in this position, and Graham never really knew – was he meant to be on Liam's side or the principal's side? He knew which side he *felt* he was on. He felt it like a ball of fire in his gut.

5 mins

'Say sorry?' Liam said.

Graham's hands flipped over so that his palms were now facing up. He shuffled forward to the edge of his chair.

'Okay. Well, that's a start,' the principal said slowly. 'How do you think you could show Martin that you are sorry, Liam?'

Graham fell back into the chair. He'd seen the school's pamphlet on redemptive justice; this was going to take a while. At the previous school, they just suspended the kid. Straightforward. Except for the strike three rule, which meant that Liam had been expelled, and none of that or anything else had been straightforward at all. They'd ended up moving house, moving everything: a fresh start. It was a bit of a drive from Jenny's mum's, but you could get a cheap rental in Mount Barker as well as a decent meat pie. Nice trees. Cinema complex. Mount Barker was okay. If Liam could just stay out of trouble. If Winners could get off the ground. Graham rolled his neck anticlockwise. This was not the way to run a new business – not being there. He turned his attention to what Liam might do in the shop for the rest of the week if he got suspended. There wasn't much he could do. Rearrange the trophies? Paint more road signs to try and direct people to the old mechanic's shop behind the disused servo on Hutchinson Street? Graham was under no illusions: Winners was in a rubbish location – you couldn't even see it from the road – but the rent was minimal. One day, Winners would be in the main street, or even Mount Barker Central. This was only for now.

And then Graham thought, Maybe Liam could man the shop while he drove Jenny down the freeway to her mum's? Kill two birds with one stone.

'Graham, what are your thoughts here?' the principal asked. 'Liam's only been at our school for six months. Yet this is the third time he's been involved in an incident with another student, where someone has been hurt by Liam's actions. What are your thoughts here, Graham?'

Graham felt himself heat up. He turned again to Liam. The way he sat slumped in the chair, with his legs splayed out in front, made the roll of fat around his middle sit up like a sponge cake. The boy needed more exercise or he'd be on the road to pre-diabetes like his mother. On the clean short carpet, his sneakers looked old and scuffed, the laces frayed and too long. Graham couldn't see his son's eyes through the hair flopped over his face. He'd thought he was the luckiest man alive to have a pigeon pair, a girl and a boy. He thought of Jenny again, probably home from TAFE by now. She was doing Certificate III in Aged Care, and in less than eight months she'd be qualified to get a job at Sevenoaks Retirement Village. They just needed to hold on until then, cash flow wise. She was trying to lose weight too. Her biggest problem was using up all her points mid-morning with a Mars Bar or Snickers and then spending the rest of the day feeling cranky. None of this seemed an appropriate match to the principal's question. Had there even been a question? Graham shrugged.

'I understand that Liam was expelled from his previous school as a result of similar behaviours. Was there any kind of intervention done then, or since?'

Graham levered himself up to a straighter position. He cleared his throat; there was a cobweb in it, snagging over the word. 'Intervention?'

'Well, I'm not suggesting there's a specific problem, what the problem might be, but I'm wondering if there's been any testing done? We've got some pretty aggressive behaviours here. Behaviours that, frankly, I'm not happy to have at my school. I think it would be good for Liam, for everyone, if we tried to get to the bottom of it.'

'Maybe Liam should spend some time at home, with me?' Graham offered. 'To cool off. Liam said it was an accident and, personally, I believe him. He's a good kid.'

Graham's eyes wandered again over his son. Sometimes looking at Liam was a bit like looking at himself, but a hidden, unknown part of himself, like an internal organ, his liver or his kidneys. It made Graham feel sentimental and protective and repulsed, all at once. He tried to focus his thoughts. Liam was a good kid. He just had a bit of growing up to do. Graham felt a sudden clarity and wash of affection.

'He always helps his mother around the house, puts out the rubbish, carries in shopping bags from the car. Rakes the leaves for his gran. He's not a bad kid. We have got his ears tested – no problems there. Excellent hearing, actually. He gets a bit overexcited, is all. Loves his *Star Wars*. Wants to be Bear Grylls. You know what boys are like.'

Graham tried to laugh but couldn't get any traction beyond the first few syllables. It often went like this; he couldn't think of anything to say, but then suddenly he could. It was like finally seeing the face in one of those swirly optical illusion paintings, the way it all came together in his mind. It occurred to him to tell the principal that Liam's great-grandfather was a light horseman in the First World War.

When Liam looked up at him and smiled, Graham wasn't sure whether he wanted to cuff his son across the head or pull him into a hug.

The suspension wasn't allowed to be like a holiday, the principal told them. And Graham had to come back to the school in the morning to collect schoolwork from Mrs Murphy. He also had to be available to supervise Liam at least till the end of the week.

Graham told the principal that, being self-employed, this

wouldn't be a problem. He added that he had his own business. The principal just nodded, ushered them out, and said, 'Right, then. Good, then.'

They pulled open the door of the front office and felt the frigid late afternoon air cut through their windcheaters.

'And, Liam,' the principal called, 'I want you to really have a think about how Martin might be feeling; not only now, but tonight, and tomorrow, and for the rest of this week.'

Liam called back over his shoulder, 'Righto.' His voice sounded light and carefree, Graham thought – exactly as though he was about to go on a holiday.

10 mins.   ~   Skip

'It's all the video games,' Jenny said later that night when they were lying awake, the wind knocking the broken awning against the side of their bedroom window. 'I saw it on *Today Tonight* – violent video games.'

'Nahsnot.' Graham rolled over to face her. He ran his hand across her hip and down her thigh. He picked up her hand and shifted her wedding band between his fingers. They'd hocked her diamond engagement ring eight months ago, right in between his job at The Potato Factory and two-week stint at the abattoir. Remembering the boning room still made him twitch. He hadn't even got to the kill floor, but he'd seen it, and those two hours he'd spent locked in the cold room had made their way into dreams. He wondered if the engagement ring would fit Jenny again now, or not quite, even if he could get it back.

'Well, Soph doesn't play those games. She doesn't bash other kids up.'

Graham laughed quietly through his nose. 'Don't be ridiculous, love.' Sophie was small and stringy and kept to herself, like him. And she was a girl.

'You should shave off that moustache,' Jenny said. 'Makes you look shonky.'

He smiled and rolled back onto his own pillow.

'Maybe we should do more things as a family,' she said. 'Maybe we should get a dog.'

Graham lay still, mulling over the bits of rope and lackey straps he'd kept from the shed at their previous place, something he could use to strap up the awning.

~

Liam sat at the front counter of Winners the next morning playing *Solitaire* on the old computer, his head resting sloppily in one hand. Graham had coached him for half an hour on answering the phone smartly but decided in the end it was best to switch the line through to his Bluetooth. Putting in the landline didn't really make any sense anyway, it just seemed more professional. But the boy's voice still hadn't broken and it didn't sound right, the way he squeaked, 'Good morning, Winners' – more like a question than a fact. It didn't really look right either, the boy in charge. Graham wondered when it would, how long it would take for him to fill out in the right places and lose the puppy fat and look like a man. Handing a thriving business over to your son must be an awesome feeling.

Graham had thought about it a lot, had even wondered about calling the shop Barlow and Sons, Trophies SA. But he did have a daughter too. She hadn't shown any interest, but she wasn't interested in anything these days, and Graham wasn't sexist. She'd come round. He'd settled on Winners when he imagined Sophie and Liam telling their school friends, 'Our dad's the manager of Winners.' When Graham first came up with the business idea, he'd imagined himself becoming a sort of identity in sporting communities. He didn't know how it would happen exactly, but when he'd had this dream, he'd pictured the Graham Barlow Award. A trophy for something – maybe not even for a sporting achievement, maybe it would be for the display of a virtue, like never giving up.

'Who's number one?' he asked his son as he pulled open the heavy glass door to leave the shop.

'I am.' Liam smiled back.

As Graham looked over his shoulder at the old petrol bowser, he saw that the set-up looked more like a garage sale than a proper business. He needed more stock, pure and simple. The opportunity to actually pick things up, handle them, feel their weight, was his point of difference with the major suppliers. He needed crystal trophies, fusion metal and acrylic, maybe some of those glass paperweights. Branching into corporate and giftware would make a lot of sense. It wasn't as if Graham lacked vision or ideas. What he lacked was capital, but his credit rating was crap. A loan for a Trotec laser engraver was what he needed most. At the moment, he'd have to send things away, not just for sand blasting but for any engraving at all. The truth was, Graham was purchasing his stock from the online competitors.

Graham left the school and wound through the back streets of town to Haydn Street where all the front lawns were overgrown and old couches grew mouldy on verandahs. As promised, Liam's teacher had left a stack of workbooks with a handwritten note. In the pile was a thin softcover book on Australian birds and, under that, a printed page from Wikipedia. Graham wondered if the teacher had assumed Liam didn't have internet at home. There'd been a couple of notes from both the kids' schools about that. If you didn't have internet access, the school would provide extra time in class. Things were tough, but he and Jenny weren't stupid. How would Sophie and Liam be able to do homework without proper internet?

He found Jenny waiting for him by their tin letterbox. She had a snarled expression on her face and a bag of oranges at her feet. 'Mum was expecting me an hour ago, Graham.' She took the pile of books from the front passenger seat and climbed awkwardly into the car. She dropped the oranges to the floor, huffing and puffing, then settled the books onto her lap. She picked up the note and smoothed her hand across the small, thin book on top. 'Bird watching,' she said. 'I used to love bird watching.'

Graham snorted as he pulled out of the driveway and back onto the road. 'Since when have you been into bird watching?'

'I used to be into bird watching, Graham.'

They were quiet for a few minutes while Jenny read Mrs Murphy's note and flicked through Liam's books.

'I reckon she thinks we don't have internet.'

Graham indicated right and merged onto the freeway.

'I'm gonna give you driving lessons.'

'I don't need driving lessons. I know how to drive.'

'I can't take a day off to drive you down to your mum's every week, Jen. I've gotta be there, at the shop. And I gotta be networking. No one knows me from a bloody bar of soap up here.'

'She needs me,' Jenny said. 'Imagine if I was all alone one day and our kids didn't come.'

A small part of Graham hoped they wouldn't. It didn't bother him that he and Jenny had never left Adelaide. There was nowhere particularly he wanted to go – Queensland, maybe – but he imagined his kids going places, doing things. For the past five years, since they were seven and nine, Graham had put money into their Bank SA student accounts. Every single fortnight. No matter how tough things were, even if it was only a dollar, and sometimes that's all it was. He felt good whenever he thought about those accounts. He liked to see his kids' names printed on the bank statements in that little window on the envelope. He wanted to believe that Winners might set them up.

~

Jenny's mum was sitting in her small cement porch on a fold-up chair.

'Well, I thought you were never coming,' she said as they got out of the car. She turned and hobbled back inside the unit, and Graham saw that she was wearing the compression tights Jenny had bought her last week. She moved like Jenny: from the hips, awkwardly swaying sideways in order to propel forward. She sat down on the floral lounge chair and sighed, laid her head on the backrest and stayed there while Jenny made cups of tea and worked through her washing.

Jenny passed Graham a load of her mother's clothes and said, 'Fold these. You're as useless as an ashtray on a motorbike, hun.'

~

On the way home, Jenny looked at Liam's homework again. Graham wondered how she managed to avoid getting carsick. She was competent, his wife, in so many ways, and it bothered him that people wouldn't know it if they only saw her in the street. He thought of her TAFE studies and the high grades she was getting for the units.

'Look, he's supposed to fill this worksheet out,' she said, and she held up one of the loose papers. 'Looks like the other kids are going bird watching on an excursion. They're all going to the Laratinga Wetlands. I never saw a form for that. Liam'll miss that.'

Graham glanced over the loose Wikipedia page Jenny was holding up. 'What's an Australasian bittern?'

'They say it's rare. Special. The icon bird of the Australian swamp. Might even be endangered.'

'And what, they reckon they've got them in the wetlands? I thought that place was for dumping the town's shit.'

Jenny slapped the page across his arm. 'It's environmental, Graham. How's he supposed to get this worksheet done if he doesn't get to go on the excursion? They're setting him up to fail, is what they're doing.'

'Well, he should bloody well do it.' Graham remembered the principal's uninterested smile as he'd steered them out of his office, as though he'd given up on Liam already. Graham pushed his palm into the steering wheel. 'There's nothing to say he can't go to the wetlands, is there? It's a free bloody country. He can just do it, and then hand in that worksheet like everyone else. That's what he'll do.'

'Yep. He could walk there. Get some exercise. We could all go. We never do anything together anymore. Remember when we used to do things all together?'

Graham remembered the time he drove them to Willunga, and they had fish'n'chips on the beach. How old was Sophie then? He wondered. Six? Seven? With that wispy blonde hair. He used to call her his little princess, back then.

~

Graham rolled the Blu-Tack around in his fingers and stuck the card back up on the front door of the shop. He switched the line to his Bluetooth and clipped it over his ear. He still hadn't heard from Troy Campbell at the Hahndorf Football Club. As he locked the door, he decided he would call again himself that afternoon. Persistence was the key. Never giving up. He had to *think* like a winner.

Liam and Jenny waited for him in the car at the petrol bowsers. Jenny had claimed she didn't mind missing TAFE if it was for bird watching. When Graham had thrown his hands in the air, she'd made her eyes big and said, 'What?' They'd offered the morning off school to Sophie too, because bird watching was educational, but she said she didn't want to go anywhere that Liam was going. Then she'd walked off down the street with her schoolbag half hanging off one shoulder, as if she might just drop it on the ground and leave it there.

Graham parked the car in the Homemaker Shopping Centre. Jenny had packed supplies: drink bottles and a collection of snacks.

'How long you planning on being here?' Graham asked.

'Well, you don't know. That's the thing about bird watching, Graham. You have to be patient.'

She and Liam were both puffing by the time they'd followed the asphalt walking trail to the first pond, flanked with native grasses that reached over their heads. There was no one much around on this Wednesday morning; an older man on a bike passed them and a couple of mums with prams. Jenny had also packed the little digital camera they'd got for taking out a *National Geographic* subscription that no one ever read, but it wasn't charged so Graham put it in his jacket pocket and got out his phone for taking pictures. Liam had the worksheet in one hand and a blue biro in the other, and he dragged his feet as he walked, so that Graham saw how his sneakers had become so scuffed.

'There, mate. That's one of those ducks.' Jenny pointed an arm vigorously toward the pond. 'The blue-billed whatsname duck. And look, there's a honeyeater. The New Holland honeyeater. Tick 'em off, Liam. Here, give me that sheet.'

Liam handed the worksheet to Jenny as if it meant nothing to him, as if he didn't even know what it was. She took the biro from him too and rested the page on the book over her thigh to tick inside the boxes.

As they walked, Jenny read from the book and Mrs Murphy's printout. She told them how the effluent treatment worked, that Laratinga was a Peramangk word for the Mount Barker Creek. She said she'd had no idea there were so many different birds in the wetlands. 'That's the thing about bird watching,' she said. 'Until you actually watch, you don't see any birds. It's like you have to know that you're watching, you have to decide, in a way, otherwise you won't see anything. You won't hear them either,' she said, 'unless you actually listen.'

Graham listened and realised that she was right. It was amazing how many different birds you could hear when you listened. He had no idea what they all were. Trills, chirps, high-pitched squeaks, whistles, low throaty variations. A white cockatoo shrieked overhead. Graham thought again about how smart Jenny was, the way she had a knack for putting things.

They walked on, Jenny leading, then Liam, then Graham following behind. Every now and then, Jenny would stop still and turn this way and that, and Liam would scuff his sneakers around at the gravelled edges. They passed the second body of water and then left the asphalt path for the unsealed trail. They wound further into the middle of the wetlands, a third pond and the boardwalk.

Liam spotted a group of blue wrens, and Jenny held a hand on her heart as they watched the tiny perfect birds flit about in the leaf litter, velvety black and the prettiest blue. Jenny found the bit in the book about blue wrens – she said they were actually called 'superb fairy-wrens' – and Graham took photos using his phone. They spotted more species of duck, a starling, lots of magpies, a group of corellas, a masked lapwing. Jenny ticked them all off. She continued reading as they walked. Sometimes she'd stop and read something aloud. There are birds, she said, that breed in Japan and Siberia and then fly all the way here to escape the northern winter.

Graham zipped up his jacket. He hadn't ever seen snow. It was early spring and you could see signs of it, especially in the wetlands, but the air still had the bite of winter. There hadn't been a stretch of sunny days or blue skies yet. He'd never carried much body fat, and the cold air nipped straight to his bones.

They didn't see any more birds for a while. Occasionally, they would think they had, but then they'd realise that one was already ticked off. Jenny said she wished they owned a pair of binoculars.

'These are all the common birds,' she said when they reached a bench and she looked over the worksheet. 'We still haven't really seen something special, something rare.'

Graham stood at the bench while Jenny and Liam sat at either end, pulling out the drinks and packs of flavoured crackers.

'Let's go back,' Liam said through a mouthful. 'This is boring.' He had flecks of orange seasoning around his lips. 'Just tick 'em off, Mum. How would she know, anyway?' He kicked at the bolts holding the bench to the ground.

The kid had a point, thought Graham. It was tempting just to tick off all the boxes. But then he thought they should see it through, as a lesson in itself. When he'd closed up the shop yesterday, he'd seen that Liam had spent the whole morning looking at porn on the computer. If he wasn't at school, then he should bloody well be doing schoolwork. It was good to make him stay and do it, to finish the task.

Right at the bottom of the worksheet was a hand-drawn sketch of the Australasian bittern. Above it, Mrs Murphy had put three question marks and an exclamation mark. It had been sighted once or twice before by some serious bird watchers – it wasn't as if it was impossible to see one, but Jenny was right; it was rare. Graham turned from the bench and surveyed the vast expanse of inky water in front of them. He checked his watch. They'd been gone for almost an hour. He tried to imagine what it would be like if they saw a bittern, if he got a picture on his phone. He imagined how excited Jenny would be, ticking the box on the worksheet and, later, attaching a copy of the photo. He imagined Liam going back to school after his suspension with that. Mrs Murphy would send him to the principal's office to show it off. No doubt they'd put Liam's worksheet up on the noticeboard at the front office and everyone would see it; all the parents and the other kids. Liam would get an A, for sure. Maybe sighting an Australasian bittern was so special that the principal would ring the *Courier* and there'd be a story about it in the local rag.

The first drop of rain hit Graham's closed mouth. As he brought his hand up to wipe it away, another hit his wrist. He turned back to the bench and saw that Jenny was stuffing the drink bottles and empty wrappers into Liam's schoolbag. She folded the worksheet in half and put that and the pen in there too. She passed Graham the bag and eased herself to her feet, leaning on Liam's knee and wobbling. The raindrops became large and random and splattered generously. Liam stood and covered his head with his hands. Another year and he'd be as tall as his mother. A breeze came up, shimmering through branches and leaves and turning them into wind chimes. A current swept across the large body of water.

Graham put both straps of the bag over his shoulders and led the way to the boardwalk.

'Shortcut to the main path,' he said and turned back to make sure his family were following.

The downpour came quickly and hard. The singular drops of rain turned suddenly into long vertical sheets of water. There was a crack of thunder over the valley.

Graham broke into a jog. He heard Jenny and Liam yell out, and turned again to see them lumbering behind him, their mouths open, hair flat and dripping against their foreheads.

'Run!' he yelled, but even as the word left his mouth and was drowned against the wall of rain, he knew that neither of them could. Carrying so much extra weight, and with that dodgy hip, Jenny was struggling to walk. All she could manage was a lopsided shuffle. Liam was slow too, and his knees seemed to collapse into each other.

On every occasion that Graham had been called up to Liam's schools, he had privately wondered if his son was even capable of the injuries he allegedly inflicted. A twisted arm that had required an X-ray, a black eye, a chipped tooth, numerous blood noses. And now Martin someone, with concussion and stitches across his left eyebrow. It didn't add up. Graham couldn't help wondering if they all just had it in for his boy, as if they wanted Liam in trouble, as if they just didn't like him.

Graham stopped on the boardwalk and waited for Liam and Jenny to catch up. The three of them stood still for a moment, soaked and helpless, unable to hear one another speak against the intensity of the rainstorm. Liam's face was pale, his teeth chattering, and Graham thought that Jenny might even be crying.

He realised then that he still had the Bluetooth around his ear. As he pulled it off and shoved it into his pocket, he knew it was ruined. He might as well have had a shower fully clothed. He wiped his hands across his face to try and see more clearly. You couldn't bring cars into the wetlands; he would have to guide them back to the Homemaker Centre at the pace they could manage. They moved slowly on, their arms wrapped around their own bodies, Graham in front, then Liam, then Jenny.

Finally, they reached the sealed path. The rain pulled back as quickly as it had started and then fell again in random, singular drops. It became strangely quiet, as if the heavens were recoiling from their own outburst. Everything around them softly ticked, like a resting engine when the ignition is cut. Graham slowed his step so that the others could catch up again, and he reached for Jenny's hand. With her gait so lopsided, it was hard to hold her hand while they walked, and he rarely did. He reached over and put his other hand on Liam's shivering shoulder. His thumb nestled in the groove above Liam's collarbone and, with his other hand wrapped around Jenny's, he could feel the racing pulses of both his wife and his son. They are alive and real, he thought. His family is alive and real. They are flesh and bone, sinew and fat. And Graham understood then that being alive meant that one day they would die, like everything else, like all these living things here. He felt a tickle in his throat and behind his eyes, and a great burden of love for them in his chest. But Jenny was right. They should have made Sophie come too. Graham realised that he missed her. He really missed her. He'd been missing her for a couple of years. He squeezed Jenny's hand and firmed his grip on Liam's shoulder. He wished he could think of something to say, words to explain how he really felt about his family. He wanted to put this feeling into words.

What he did know was this: Liam's school could get stuffed. Troy Campbell could get stuffed. The whole world could go and get stuffed. Jenny was right. They needed to do more things as a family.

They continued walking the last stretch of the path, almost back to the Homemaker Centre. All Graham could hear now was the rasping breathlessness of his wife and son beside him, and the odd chirp of all those unknown birds as they ventured timidly back out into the open.

WORLD PEACE

Janis has had it – evidence, she supposes – in her skirt pocket since Tuesday. Now it's Wednesday. One night and nearly two days in her pocket. She can *feel* it. Scrapes against her thigh every time she moves and sort of even tickles.

There is nothing so bad you can't tell someone. Megan said that and then stared at her so hard, Janis just nodded to make it stop. But Megan is wrong: just another one of those things that grown-ups say and you can tell that they read it somewhere first. On a pamphlet probably, like the one about cyber safety from the Australian Federal Police.

Some thoughts are best left as thoughts. They should stay in people's heads. It's one thing to think something, another to put that thing into actual words and another to write those words down. That means write with a pen, type or text. *Leave those thoughts in your head! Please!* And probably see a psychologist or something. Because now Janis practically needs to see one. Just because someone didn't.

It's a letter, in her pocket. Handwritten on paper. The paper is folded into a tight square the size of a twenty-cent piece. Hard and grubby. Janis can barely think straight, knowing it's there. It's very stressful. Ever since yesterday, the words in this letter have been going around and around in her brain, swirling about like actual objects, like the origami cranes hung with fishing line from their classroom ceiling. They're supposed to make one thousand to send to Hiroshima, for world peace. Janis can't see it happening.

If Mrs Marveed or Mr Everett ever saw what was written in this letter – Janis doesn't want to think about it. Or Mrs Sheena? *Foul.* Janis has that butterfly feeling in her stomach like you get if there's a paedophile, and you don't feel *comfortable.* And her mouth is dry. She's practically got all the Early Warning Signs. She wonders about the girl in the news, whether she had any. And if she did, at what point she got them. Janis wonders about the order that everything happened, the timeline they showed, from when she went missing and when they found the backpack and everything else, and she gets another sign – a shiver, it literally goes through her whole body. And then she remembers that Megan will want to wash her school skirt tonight. She always does – it's Wednesday and Janis is meant to be going to her dad's, which means not only is she going to have to talk to the stupid lady from the Bureau of Meteorology, she's also going to have to think of something to do with the letter in her pocket. Fast! – like, today.

The letter is from Jaydan. To Maddie B – Janis's best friend. Janis can hardly look at Jaydan.

Okay, so Sarah knows about it too, because Janis had to

do *something* to make her realise that the thing with Martin is nothing. Compared to this. Sarah was worried she might end up on Martin's bully audit because she called him a dork. She said it was an accident. Janis doesn't know how you could accidently call anybody anything. Compared to this, Sarah's got nothing to worry about. Sarah needs to chill out. Martin *is* a dork, but that's not the point. If you get on more than one person's bully audit or on the same person's more than twice, you have to go and talk with Mrs Sheena. You don't get in that much trouble but it's annoying because afterwards you feel yucky. And Janis hates – *hates* – that feeling. No one says much after they've been to Mrs Sheena. Janis has only been once, with a group of girls last year, and just thinking about it makes her feel a bit wrong.

Oceania's left now, anyway. What kind of name is Oceania? She said her dad had a job somewhere else and they had to move, but Janis and the girls knew it was because she didn't have any friends. And Maddie G saw her at Mount Barker Woolworths a week ago, so they musn't've moved far. Oceania was always dobbing, for the stupidest things. Even the teachers found her annoying, they just couldn't admit it – the girls could always tell if the teachers liked someone or not.

Not that 'Janis' is a much better name. She is named after Janis Joplin, which is totally embarrassing. She'll change it at Births, Deaths and Marriages. This is partly why she has started calling her mum 'Megan', to rub it in that she got a normal name and yet decided to give her daughter a stupid weird one. The other girls have started doing it too, calling their mums by their first names, which some of the mums hate. It's sort of a craze.

4 mins .

36

Martin basically thinks he's a girl, and it drives the girls nuts. Savannah called him a he/she yesterday, which Janis has never heard of before, but it's a good description of Martin – hangs around with girls, can't play footy, always wants to do what the girls are doing, even though he is actually a boy.

Sarah was thinking about going out with him, just for a day, so he wouldn't put her on his audit. Janis said 'no', as in, 'No!' Martin Wheeler has been in her class for two years now, and Janis knows what he would do. He would think Sarah *really* likes him, and then he'd follow her around for weeks like a puppy dog. The way Lachlan follows Janis, which is so annoying. The way Jaydan *used* to follow Maddie B.

But Martin would never write anything like the stuff that's in this letter. That's a plus for Martin, she supposes.

'Actually,' Janis said, thinking of her own dog, 'that's like an insult to puppies.' Sarah agreed. Janis loves Bella even though she's not a puppy anymore. She's a little terrier cross. Megan's boyfriend, Dan, calls her 'the mutt' or 'muttonhead', in a mean way. Just because Janis and Megan don't know what Bella's crossed with. Janis loves the way Bella lies over a pillow like a black-and-white banana with her head flopped on the floor. Sometimes, Janis lies down next to her and puts her face right up to Bella's wet nose. Megan says it's revolting, and Dan says the mutt will bite her face off, but Janis knows that Bella never would. Here's what's revolting: Dan cuts up cows and sheep at the abattoir for a job.

Some things Janis just knows. She didn't have to read them anywhere or have someone tell them to her. She knows that Bella would never, ever bite her. She knows, absolutely, that Sarah and Maddie B (not G!) are her best friends. Some boys are cute (Austin) but most of them are annoying. She will never get married. She hates Dan – it's not her fault that he's Megan's boyfriend. She hates Dan as much as she hates Jaydan. (Dan/Jay-dan. *Not surprising!*) Even though her dad left Megan for the stupid lady at the Bureau of Meteorology – Sylvie – he's the best dad. (She wishes they weren't having the baby, though. Would stop it, if she could. They've even picked the name, and Janis hates it and is jealous of it, and that feels like one feeling, not two.) Certain things are best kept in your head and should never be written down on paper or typed into anything.

But some things Janis doesn't know. After the tickling feeling there is a huge black hole, and what would happen if you were to fall in? And if something feels right and wrong and good and bad, which one is it?

~

So how did Janis end up with this letter in her pocket? It's not like it's even meant for her. The short version is that Maddie made her take it. This is what happened. In a timeline.

- Jaydan and Maddie were going out for like, two weeks (ages). He got Austin to ask her.
- Something happened in the computer suite with Maddie and Jaydan at recess (still Monday) but she won't tell Janis what, even though she's supposed to be her best friend.
- Maddie told Jaydan she didn't want to go out with him

anymore. (Still Monday.) He called her a slut on Kik. She said fuck off. *Blah-blah-blah.*

- In the middle of German (now *Tuesday)* Maddie opens her German 1 textbook and finds this folded up piece of paper, this *letter.*
- Maddie reads it and her face goes white. She literally pushes it into Janis's hand.
- Janis reads the letter. *Oh My God.* She doesn't know what half of it means (she doesn't tell Maddie this). She doesn't know what to say. She puts it in the pocket of her skirt because there's a zip and she knows it won't fall out. Mistake.
- Maddie won't take the letter back and keeps crying in the girls' toilets.
- The letter stays in Janis's skirt pocket the whole night and all today (Wednesday).
- Janis doesn't know what to do with it because she doesn't want it either. And now, it's nearly home time.

A lot of other things happened in between all those things but with a timeline you only stick to the facts, not all the details or how you felt. Janis wonders if she should give the letter to the police. Anonymously, like they said.

They had the special assembly last Friday. Two police officers came, a man and a lady – she was tall and skinny, really pretty. After, they had to break up into forum groups and talk about it.

Janis might be a policewoman one day.

There are so many e-crimes you could do. Cyber stalking,

phishing, cyber bullying, sexting, all these things. Some of them you could even do without realising it. Because what people forget is this: once you've written it, it actually doesn't go away. Ever. Which is why there's tip number four in the top ten tips for cyber safety – Think before you send! – practically exactly Janis's point about keeping things in your head. Because, there's computer forensics. Computer forensics is how they found the man who killed that girl. Janis can't remember her name right now, but she remembers liking the sound of it. Sophie Someone. It was the name of a girl you'd want to be friends with. It had a feel to it, Janis remembers, like a good song. They found her backpack first.

Because she's dead. That girl is dead. He kept her for twelve days before he killed her. Twelve days. Twelve. Janis can put that in perspective; she is twelve. Twelve is a long time.

But the police failed to mention what people can do with a pen and paper, didn't talk about it once.

So what is Janis supposed to do? Does she ring Crime Stoppers?

~

Wednesdays go like this – Megan picks her up from school, she gets changed, has something to eat, packs her fluffy owl et cetera, then Megan drops her off at Jazz. Then her dad picks her up from Jazz and she stays at his house in Hahndorf until Saturday. Then they reverse it because she's got Hip-Hop on Saturday.

Janis's dad works at the Bureau of Meteorology, which is part of the Department of Sustainability, Environment, Water,

Population and Communities. His name is Terry. People might have heard of him, but they probably haven't. He was on television for four seconds when they were talking about the drought, ages ago. He was on in the background, on the Systems Help Desk. With Sylvie.

'*Yes, yes, I'll marry you. I'll marry you,*' she heard her dad whisper hard into a wall one day. And then she saw he was on his mobile. And she thought, That's weird – isn't he already married? To Mum?

~

Megan is stressed. Janis has hardly finished getting changed, and she's being told to hurry, hurry. 'Look,' Megan says, 'I haven't had time to do a proper shop. Damn the heating in this house.' She's right – it's freezing, and it's meant to be spring. 'But I got you an apricot danish from Brezel's,' she calls out. She's walking down the hallway. 'It's on the kitchen bench.'

A white paper bag. Janis used to love the white paper bags with the yellow sticky tape. She partly still does. It's just that danishes actually make you fat.

Megan is running around somewhere. She's never still anymore. Even when Janis is trying to tell her something, she doesn't look at her properly.

Then she yells: 'Honestly!'

And that's when Janis realises what room her mother is in. Janis has a mouthful of danish when she realises it. That aeroplane-taking-off sound of the washing machine, and Megan's heels ticking on the tiles.

Her mum is doing the washing. Janis can't breathe. The letter. Pastry turns to paste on her tongue. She was going to work out what to do with the letter *before* she put her skirt in the laundry. She was going to work it out while she was eating the apricot danish! She puts the danish down and sits there, frozen. Her heart is beating so fast it feels like someone is tap-dancing inside her chest.

'Can you come here, please?' Megan's voice is wobbly and sharp.

Janis stands. Someone has dropped a house on her head. She walks slowly to the laundry.

Her mum is holding the little folded square up to Janis's face, between her thumb and her pointy finger. The letter that will probably put Jaydan in jail. *Jay-dan! Jay-il!* All the words jump around in her head and won't sit still. *Oh God!*

'Really?' Megan says. 'What is this?' There is a crazy look in her eye as though she is seeing Janis and not seeing Janis, as though Janis exists and as though she doesn't. As though Janis isn't even standing there.

Then her mum lifts up her other hand and presents a ball of tissue. The one, in fact, that Janis had offered to Maddie to blow her nose with.

Janis can't speak. She doesn't have a plan for what to say. Her brain is bursting with so many different things, so many different people: there's Mrs Sheena, Mrs Marveed, Mr Everett, there's Maddie's mum, the skinny police lady, Jaydan, his mum and dad. Is there really a kid's jail? She doesn't even know how this is going to work. She assumes there'll have to be some kind of investigation. Maddie is going to have to talk about what happened in the computer suite on Monday.

'Honestly.'

Her mum reaches down and lifts up Janis's hand. She squashes the letter and the tissue into it. Why does everyone keep giving it to *her*?

'I've told you before,' her mum says, her voice wobbling again, 'this is the stuff that makes lint. You've got to empty your pockets. These are the things, Janis.' She huffs the air out again, and then she grabs a pair of Dan's pants from the laundry basket and digs her hands into the pockets. Paper receipts, a bit of scrunched-up paper towel with black stuff on it – grease? Another tissue – it's like a magic trick, and she's throwing it all around the laundry. 'These are the things!' she yells. Megan has lost it. Janis gets it – she already hates Dan.

Janis considers telling Megan that she had planned to empty the pocket (like, she'd been thinking about nothing else for two days!) but instead she closes her hand around the tissue and the letter and tries to control her mouth. Her eyes are blinking too fast, and she's having trouble slowing them down. She says: 'Sorry.'

She walks back to her bedroom. She can hear Megan crying in the laundry. The door clicks behind her, and she sits on the bed. It feels as though brakes are screeching and grating inside her. She opens her hand and starts to unfold the letter, her hands shaking. Weirdly, she has an urge to read it again. Just to feel how grateful she is. She wants to feel this brand of gratefulness because she knows it's not the kind you might feel if someone gives you a present. It's completely different to that; it's heavy.

Maddie's rejected tissue is still in her hand too, and she chucks it over her bed into her plastic IKEA bin.

The bin. Oh God. She is such an idiot. Such a total idiot.

The unfolded letter is lying flat in her lap, thin wrinkles all through it like an old person's face. It's not even that big – probably just the bottom third ripped from a piece of lined A4 paper. Blue biro – a BIC, probably. She doesn't read the words, she *sees* them, lines and loops and dots and swirls. She rips the paper into two. She closes her eyes and opens them. And then rips again. And then again, and she can't stop. She is like a crazy lady ripping this letter into the tiniest pieces you could imagine, and then she cups her hands and looks at what she's done. Tiny pieces of paper dotted with little specks of blue. She leans over her bed and shapes her hands into a funnel. The pieces float down into the bin like confetti. Such an idiot.

She – *honestly* – doesn't know why she didn't think of this before. And now she wants to laugh out loud, and she wishes she could but it won't come. It's like someone has physically picked her up off the floor. So, she hasn't got the evidence anymore. But she doesn't even care. Now that it's gone, all of it seems stupid. The whole thing. She stands up and walks over to her dresser.

Janis has this thing she does where she stares at herself in the mirror for ages without blinking and tries to imagine that, if she concentrates hard enough, maybe she could lift off the ground, even if only by a couple of inches. The smallest start to flying. She might have already done it – she thinks she has. One day she imagines she'll go higher and hover at the ceiling. And then another day, she will slide her bedroom window across and go, just take off. She'll sit in a holding pattern above the treetops for a while, and people will see her and point and be in awe. And then she'll kick off and fly away, probably for good.

Her skin is all shiny, too shiny. There's a new pimple on the side of her nose. It's not that big, but she's not very pretty. Not as pretty as Savannah or Sarah or even Maddie B.

Megan opens the door. Bella charges in even though she's not allowed, but Megan doesn't say anything. She actually looks horrible. Her eyes are red, and there's black stuff on her cheeks. Mascara. She says, 'Look, it's got nothing to do with you. Sorry. We have to get going.' A sob comes out of her like a sneeze or a cough would come out of someone else. She pulls herself back to tall and holds up her hands like she's about to give an important speech and wants the clapping to stop. Janis puts her hand under her pillow and pulls out fluffy owl.

Wednesday. Sylvie will be at the pregnancy yoga thing. It'll just be Janis and her dad. They'll have their usual – spinach and ricotta ravioli with Dolmio pasta sauce. Then Golden North ice-cream with strawberry topping. Thursday, she will go on a diet.

She lies awake for ages that night. Can't sleep. Ate too much and can't stop thinking about the letter. How easy it was to get rid of. She will never forget this: if it's on paper, you can end it. You can *kill* it. But if you type words into a computer or a mobile phone, well, that's different. Even if you threw your computer off a cliff and into the sea, they could probably still get those words. Not with paper, though. Paper you can destroy.

Janis will never write anything anywhere. She will keep all of it in her head.

~

At school on Thursday, Janis tells Maddie what she did. Maddie rolls her bottom lip under her top lip and clamps down. Janis tells her it's gone. That it's all over. Maddie looks like she doesn't believe it. She says, 'Anyway. Yeah. Still.'

Not even 'thank you'.

Janis looks across the classroom through all the Harmony Day posters and dot paintings and *Imagine If* collages and the Hiroshima paper cranes, and she sees Sarah. She'll hang out with her at recess and lunch today.

Hot air is blaring out of the air-conditioning vents, and the paper cranes sway sideways and bob up and down. Only two hundred and fifty-three, and they're meant to send them next Thursday. As if. It's not going to happen. The teacher's voice drones on from somewhere in the room. Janis zones out, narrowing her eyes so that the swirling coloured cranes merge into one hypnotic blur.

She could just come back into this classroom at lunch and rip those two hundred and fifty-three cranes down, shred them until you wouldn't even know what they were. She could put them in one of those wheelie bins in the playground that don't open properly so that you can't put a big thing in – like a bomb, or a baby maybe.

No world peace then, she thinks.

RAISING BOYS

Malcolm took the bins to the top of the driveway later than usual. He'd waited until there was nothing left to do: his son was tucked in bed, lunches for the next day packed, computer shut down, and the dog fed and toileted. Mary's blue and yellow bins were already sitting at the top of her driveway, pristine and equidistant. He imagined her dragging them up the driveway alone, and he felt slightly queasy. But there they were, solid and real, like two full stops at the end of the line. It wasn't that he didn't want to take up Mary's bins – they were so light, she barely generated rubbish – he was happy to do it, he'd been doing it every Tuesday night for nearly three years.

It was right here, six weeks ago today, that Malcolm had inadvertently held Mary in his arms. She'd followed him up the driveway as he'd pulled her bins behind him. At the top, she'd wept, which had shocked him, and then, distressed and disoriented, she'd flailed toward him. He'd stepped forward as if to catch her, and his arms rose intuitively to give some sort of comfort, and for a moment their bodies softened together, absorbed fleeting, intimate knowledge. Mary was mothballs and talcum powder, and flesh that was both soft and firm, testifying to decades of gentle garden stretching and thousands of Kingstons, Monte Carlos and Orange Creams, an extra one with every cup of tea since Ron had died. Malcolm remembered her trembling against him as she told him that the dog's barking had become so bad during the day, she felt as though someone was shouting at her every time she walked out of her house. Shouting from *his* backyard.

'I can't stand it anymore,' Mary had cried, Malcolm's palm resting on her back. 'It's got so bad, I can't ... I can't go into my garden anymore.'

Moisture had seeped through his shirt where her nose hit his chest.

'I didn't want to say anything,' she'd said, 'because I know,' her voice tremulous, 'how much the boy loves the dog.' Mary only ever referred to Malcolm's son as 'the boy'. 'But I won't cope if it goes on like this. I know I won't cope.' She had looked up at him then with a weak smile and wet, filmy eyes.

~

Only the master bedroom light was still on in the house. Malcolm stood in the doorway. His wife was sitting on the edge of their bed, picking at something on her heel.

'Bins are up,' he said. She nodded absentmindedly.

'I didn't take Mary's up tonight.'

Theresa looked at him. 'Oh, for God's sake, Malcolm.' She

stood from the bed and ran her hands roughly through her recently layered hair. She turned to look at him, and he felt his facial muscles contract. She said his name again, more urgently, as if trying to rouse him from unconsciousness, but then her voice dropped and became lazy. 'Oh,' she said, 'you're so ...'

He watched her closely, his eyes widening for what, but Theresa looked away, started collecting her clothes ready for the next day: black pants and a shirt – she'd put all her skirts in the Salvos bin on the weekend after one of the boys had pointed out her ankles on yard duty.

Normally – Malcolm knew well after almost thirteen years of marriage – Theresa didn't mince words or leave them hanging like that. She wasn't afraid to call a spade a spade. It was one of the things he'd found appealing about her in the beginning.

He began unlacing his tan Florsheim shoes with a heaviness that extended into his fingertips. Had he let both of them down – his wife *and* his son? He *knew* he'd let Mary down: truth be known, he was thinking of little else. Mary's pained, tear-stained face was constantly in his thoughts. Six weeks ago he'd told her that he would fix the barking problem. He remembered the way he had cupped his hands authoritatively around her shoulders and said, 'Oh, Mary, I'm so sorry. I had no idea. This is not acceptable.' And then: 'Listen, I'll fix it. *We'll* fix it.' His son's dog was not more important than the wellbeing of an elderly widow.

He recalled her small palm against his chest, as though she were taking the pulse of his oath. And the way she'd pressed firmly against his sternum, more firmly than he'd thought her capable.

But that was six weeks ago, and he *hadn't* fixed it.

~

Malcolm hadn't wanted Jasper in the first place. He didn't think they had the time, or even the knowledge, to keep a dog. He hadn't really engaged with it, beyond stepping out of the way as it tore past him and down their hallway. He'd heard it bark – a high-ranged, irritating yelp – but never for long, he realised, because one of them would promptly let it back into the house and it would stop. According to Mary, when he and Theresa were at work, and Martin was at school, the barking was unrelenting, methodical, maddening.

~

Malcolm was reluctant to get into bed, afraid to feel the curve of Theresa's back against him, the hint of her thighs tucked away from him. He had started, for the first time in his life, to dream. The dreams were like nothing he might have hoped for. 'Of course you dream,' Theresa had told him, 'you just don't *remember* your dreams,' as if this was some kind of failing.

Malcolm knew that Theresa was tired of hearing about Mary and the problems with Jasper. She said he was *over thinking*. But he lay awake wondering if all the barking had made Mary ill. He wondered if he should ring the number for her niece, Susan. Pencilled in wobbly capitalised handwriting on the back of an unwanted business card, the number had been magnetised to Malcolm's refrigerator for the past two years. Malcolm had never had reason to call it. He'd never met Susan, just seen her twice, watering the petunias when Mary had gone on the *QE11* cruise ship. Susan's cursory watering had [...] him, rushing while the twins sat strapped and swelte[...] the back of her idling Hyundai, and he'd considered po[...]g over himself in the evening to do it properly. But he and Mary hadn't been so close back then. He hadn't given her eggplants or his famous plum jam, and they'd not yet synchronised their watering of seedlings or discussed the town – how quickly Mount Barker became the topic of all their conversations – the appropriateness of the estate entrance, the new industrial and residential developments, or the 'youth', lurking in and around them. They hadn't yet propagated their phrase, 'society today'. Malcolm was still to experience the quiet satisfaction of hearing Mary quote back tiny facts and stats that he himself had not long ago quoted to her, gleaned from news websites mostly, fuelling her suspicions and prejudices, but somehow, he imagined, contributing to her quality of life – providing her with things on which to ruminate privately. This was before Mary would nod and smile, pat the top of his hand with the palm of hers, and remind him fondly, 'But not everyone is like you, Malcolm' – triggering a rushing calm of *rightness* to which he would become addicted. 'No coincidence they put the new police station in Mount Barker,' Mary would say at the end of every one of these discussions. It would become her signature signing off.

But now all this was gone, and in its place was something hostile and cold. It sat heavily on Malcolm's chest as he tried to drop into the reprieve of sleep. The supercilious tone of Trish, the woman from Dog Whisperers, trailed across his mind. He'd phoned right after Mary's meltdown at the top of the driveway, but then not followed up. It had seemed an exorbitant amount of money, and he delayed over the decision to pay the extra $400 plus GST for the lifetime guarantee.

'The thing you have to remember,' Trish had said on the phone, 'is that dogs are pack animals.' She'd emphasised 'pack' and paused for effect. 'You have to show them who the leader is, Malcolm, and I'd say that that's you. You're the leader.'

Quite apart from the problem with the dog, and this ensuing unremitting guilt, Malcolm *missed* Mary. He simply missed her. Missed her like he missed his mother's perfect pavlova roll with whipped cream and tinned passionfruit. It wasn't just that his neighbour had stopped talking to him; it wasn't just the talking he missed. It occurred to Malcolm that she no longer even looked at him. No wave, no smile, no nod, no glance in his direction: nothing. Somehow, Mary's presence was gone. Dwelling on this made him sad but also awkward and strangely constricted, like the childhood memory of wearing a skivvy, or as if his skin had been badly sunburnt.

He turned on the pillow and turned again, tried going over the supply orders for work the next day, but sleep eluded him for another two hours. Forty-one years ago his grandfather had said, disappointment undisguised, that Malcolm was 'not really a man's man'. Malcolm knew it to be true.

~

Steve Biddulph was the easiest person to blame, not only for the problem with the dog, but for other things too. For no logical reason, Malcolm found himself searching for him, for a picture of him. It was Friday evening, and Theresa had driven Martin to scouts. With his wife and son gone, Malcolm was almost alone in the house – Jasper lay sleeping across Martin's unmade bed. He'd asked Martin to make it before he'd left, but his son had shrugged his bony shoulders. 'Jas likes it like that,' he'd said, with not a trace of rebellion or belligerence.

Malcolm hadn't actually read Biddulph's book, though he'd let Theresa believe that he had, let her believe that they were on the *same page*. His resistance had felt physical, not altogether conscious.

Malcolm scanned the bookshelf in the study, past Theresa's maths texts and teaching guides, their Aubrey–Maturin series, the Readers' Digest Atlases, and a collection of still unread books feverishly pressed into their hands over the years by Malcolm's sister Pippa – *My Place*, *The God of Small Things* and others – until *The Secret of Raising Happy Children* and, next to that, *Raising Boys*.

Over three million copies worldwide, Theresa had told him, that's how many Steve Biddulph books have been sold. They were selling them at the big private school for boys she was teaching at now, down in the city; she'd finally got Senior Maths and Chem. Theresa wanted Martin to go there next year, for a fresh start, but Malcolm thought it was a bad idea. You shouldn't move your child's school because you'd changed jobs and it would be convenient, or simply because you got a discount.

'It's not about convenience,' Theresa had said. 'When has it ever been about convenience?'

Malcolm pulled *Raising Boys* from its wedged position in the bookshelf. He flicked through the pages, creating a fan and a small puff of air. A number of pages were dog-eared and, stuck inside one, he found a yellow post-it note with 'class sizes?' and underneath that, 'vegemite', both in Theresa's almost illegible handwriting.

Malcolm was ninety per cent sure that this book was the source of Theresa's wrestling obsession, the fuel for her fixation with *jostling*, for the acquisition of the dog.

~

It was a Saturday. Theresa had dropped Martin at a swimming lesson. Her keys had crashed onto the kitchen bench so that Malcolm, who was bent over the dishwasher trying to dislodge the filter, stood quickly and lost his glasses into the murky overflow. His wife had put her hands on her hips.

'They *jostle*!' she'd said. 'Siblings! That's what they do. That's what siblings do. I saw it at the swimming centre. You see it all the time.'

It was his wife's eureka moment. Their son, she'd argued, never got jostled. And this was the missing ingredient, the reason he didn't have friends, or muscle tone, the reason the teachers smiled the way they did at parent–teacher interviews.

Martin was eleven – though he looked considerably younger; it had been years since they'd discussed having another child, argued about it. Out of nowhere, Theresa was making it sound as though *Malcolm* was the reason they'd stopped their family at one. 'Well,' she started saying, 'I guess this is another reason why people want siblings for their children. This is why they don't stop at one, Malcolm. You see?'

It was like she was trying to alter history. It was illogical and unsettling hearing Theresa talk like that. Because it was Malcolm who had wanted a second child, right from the beginning. Even a third. Secretly, he had hoped for a daughter. He imagined having a daughter would be like growing something magnificent, beyond your own limitations and understandings, like a rare lily or an exotic orchid.

Every time there was a new episode of bullying, or behaviour that seemed maybe odd or slightly out of kilter, 'this is why people don't stop at one, Malcolm' would rush headlong into his thoughts, the cadence straight from the mouth of his wife.

Theresa had said it was essential that Malcolm and Martin wrestle, regularly, so that Martin would understand boundaries and learn how to be a man.

'Do you have to learn how to be a man?' Malcolm had asked her. 'Don't you just grow into one?'

Malcolm didn't want to wrestle and, as far as he could see, neither did his slight and ungainly son, whose temperament and inclination were those of a pacifist. The boy was a magnet to school bullies. Was Malcolm supposed to teach his son to fight? Is that what it was really all about? He winced as he recalled the afternoon he tried to initiate wrestling, for Theresa's benefit. He'd grabbed Martin unawares into a sort of headlock while ruffling his hair with his spare hand. A misunderstanding quickly ensued, a confusion of elbows, hands and heads. Only by evening, finally, had normal behaviour resumed; Malcolm sat reading the *Advertiser* in his recliner, Martin lay on the couch playing his DS Lite, a cold blue SurgiPack draped over his right shoulder.

The dog had been her final idea. Groodles were friendly and fun, she'd said, and buying a grown, trained dog meant that they could bypass everything pertaining to a puppy. It would be Martin's dog, so he would have naming rights as well as all the responsibilities of dog ownership.

Malcolm fanned through the pages of *Raising Boys* again and then flipped it over. Disturbingly, Steve Biddulph's author photograph on the back cover was like looking at a picture of himself, down to stupid specific details like his glasses frames. What he wanted to know was this: what could this man possibly know about raising boys, about men? Not one of those three million people who had bought these books had ever wondered this? He studied the photograph and tried to imagine how Steve Biddulph would fix the problem with the dog. Resentment bubbled in his chest. He rubbed his palm across his throat.

~

Malcolm's second attempt at a solution had been to lock Jasper in the laundry while he and Theresa were at work and Martin was at school. Mother and son had both said 'no': locking up a dog eleven hours a day, five days a week was cruel. What if he needed to go outside? A dog flap was out of the question; all of the backyard doors were sliding glass ones.

'How can it be cruel,' Malcolm had said to Theresa, who was filling the kettle in the kitchen, 'when an old lady can't even come out of her own house anymore? Can't spend time in her own garden? She says Jasper barks at her when she's out the back at the clothesline, or out the front. She can't even walk to her own letterbox to collect the mail without being tormented by our dog.'

Theresa said she found it very hard to believe that Jasper's barking was really as bad as all that.

Another week had gone by with Malcolm hiding marrowbones in the garden and rubber toys stuffed with liver, another of propping wooden crates along the fence in a bid to inhibit the dog's sightlines. When Malcolm had knocked on Mary's front door to ask if things had improved, she wouldn't answer. He'd walked the few metres back to his own house and never felt so alone.

~

Malcolm tossed *Raising Boys* across his desk and Googled 'barking dogs' again, unearthing the quagmire of contradictory and confusing advice with which he was already familiar. This time, most unsettling of all was the article he found on noise-induced autonomic imbalance trauma. *For those who are severely lacking in resilience*, it said, *just a little noise forcibly projected into their last refuge can bring them quickly to breaking point.*

Malcolm knew that Mary's last refuge was her garden. And he knew it was the reason she and Ron had bought in Gladeview Park estate six years ago – to find refuge from all the noise in town, from all the hooligans and cars and carry on. Everything was different now, Mary had told him as she'd knelt on her weeding cushion at the fence line, not like it was when Ron was the only optometrist in Mount Barker. Now there was an OPSM and a Blink and that one on the corner. Who knew how many actual optometrists were working in town now? There wasn't the care anymore, the personal attention, like people got with Ron. Everything had changed. Now it was all about two for one, Mary had told him.

Malcolm shut the computer down. It was because of him that Mary didn't feel safe in her last refuge. It wasn't the barking dog – it was Malcolm. Because he was the adult, at the end of the day, who was responsible for Jasper.

And then it dawned on him. *He* was 'society today'.

The dog would have to go.

~

Malcolm barely slept again that night and, when he did, he dreamt chaotic and dark scenarios that replayed in his mind the next day, causing him confusion about what was real and what wasn't. The missing local schoolgirl, Sophie Barlow, was there. She was wearing a school dress and a grey jumper, and in the dream she looked innocent but titillating as well, and Malcolm didn't know if this was his impression in the dream or somebody else's. '*I'm so close*,' she said in his dream, '*I'm so close*,' as though trying to guide him to her whereabouts, but it felt sexual too, and wrong. But then he dreamt of the newspapers he'd read saying that they'd found the dead body of the girl and arrested her killer, and Malcolm was unsure then, even though he was dreaming, about what was real and what he was making up.

Susan was in the dream too, shrieking at him from her aunt's backyard fence and shaking her fist like a cartoon character. '*She's got hypertension*,' Susan yelled, '*and chronic depression and muscle-contraction something*.' Even in his dream – he supposed he was having the lucid variety now – Malcolm was sure that this had come straight from the article he'd read online, but when he woke late on Saturday morning, he wasn't sure; maybe Mary did have noise-induced trauma.

~

Saturday marked the third weekend of spring. Malcolm opened his eyes to find Theresa setting down a cup of tea on his bedside table. It had been months since either of them had done something like that. His wife was already dressed in her gardening clothes. Malcolm propped himself on an elbow and sipped the tea, tentative and grateful, as if he were recovering from surgery or from having witnessed something violent.

'Let's get into the front garden today,' Theresa said. 'There are weeds coming up everywhere, even through that ground cover.' She scrunched her nose and rubbed at it roughly with the back of her hand. He wanted to smooth his hands down her legs. He wanted to draw circles with his fingers across her belly. He wanted her to lie on the bed and sink into him. He couldn't remember the last time they'd made love. It wasn't months, but it was definitely weeks. Theresa drew the curtains and sunlight flooded their bedroom.

~

An hour later, Malcolm saw that she was right. The rain of the previous weekend and a few days of sunshine during the week, and the rye grass was nearly knee-high. God, it was relentless how fast it grew, even with all that creeping saltbush. Malcolm thought nostalgically of their previous house down in Adelaide, with its paved 400-square metre block. He bent down to wrap his gloved hand around the base of an ugly and unfamiliar plant covered in fine, sharp filaments. But then, among the rye grass and spread of this nastier weed, Malcolm saw that there were scores of daffodils poking through too, most still tightly wrapped, but a good number in full flower. He stood back and looked at the garden again, focusing this time just on the daffodils, and then squinting his eyes and only seeing yellow. He pulled his focus back again and took in the bigger picture – all of it – the warm sunshine; the daffodils; his wife kneeling nearby in this insanely fertile earth; her floppy white hat concealing all but her small focused chin; the green hills across the valley. Something began to descend on him that felt warm and calming. He took a full, deep breath to try to store some of it for later.

Glancing over to Mary's front garden he saw that, by comparison, hers was completely weed free. Small clusters of orange miniature marigolds interspersed with beds of white pansies managed to grow lifeless in dark, flat mulch – she must have been getting someone in to spray glyphosate again. They'd discussed this months ago, and he'd suggested maybe glyphosate was the reason blue wrens flitted about in his backyard and not hers: maybe the weed killer took out all the interesting bugs and worms loved best by birds. He could tell

Mary had been unconvinced of his theory. She'd drawn in her bottom lip and squinted her eyes, gazed hard at the gleaming little birds darting about in leaf litter and alighting on twigs only on his side, as though even the blue wrens were part of an unjust conspiracy.

All her shrubs had been pruned hard. All that remained of the buddleias were thick, sparse sticks. Malcolm's eyes tracked along to his own back fence where the same species sprouted wide fountains of grey-green foliage and spent purple flowers, hanging heavy at their tips.

Behind him, the front door opened and Martin appeared, still in his SpongeBob pyjamas. His son's skinny ankles and wrists protruded from the hemlines in a way that made you wonder whether it was him or the pyjamas that were ill-fitting.

Jasper arrived noisily at the back gate and started to bark as an unfamiliar woman passed slowly by, another neighbour presumably on her morning walk. Malcolm looked over to Mary's garden again and felt his jaw clamp as the dog's barking quickly became rhythmic and high-pitched.

Martin trotted over to the gate on his toes, shushing the dog in his shrill voice. He looked back to Malcolm, almost lost his balance and sat down cross-legged on the concrete path at the gate. The dog stopped barking and pushed its nose through the gap between the gate and the wall, and into Martin's neck. The boy giggled, sounding, Malcolm thought, more like a girl, and much younger than eleven. He watched his son close his eyes and lean in closer so that the dog could nuzzle him. He watched his son laugh as Jasper licked maniacally over his mouth and chin and across to his ears. Malcolm stood staring, wondering if the dog had ever been wormed, and noticing, as though he were seeing Martin as a stranger might, the extent and significance of his son's crooked teeth. He mentally added braces to his financial checklist.

And then a picture flashed unexpectedly across his mind, of his son. He saw Martin suddenly, in the future, older, with straight teeth and a straight back, tall and strong and happy. Malcolm tried to grab at it, to hold the picture steady, but something else caught his eye.

Theresa was watching him. She had stood up and was smiling at him in a way that said, *See? See how the dog loves the boy? How the boy loves the dog?* The only sound now the joyful giggling of their son.

And Malcolm thought that maybe he did see. He felt a shift inside himself, the arrival of something different and new.

He knew the dog had to stay.

He would ring the number for Dog Whisperers again. They would pay for the lifetime guarantee. He would ask the woman called Trish to come and help them retrain the dog, to stop the barking. It was so simple and clear.

Malcolm would call first thing Monday. Then he would write Mary a note and put it in her letterbox. The note would explain the arrangements and then, soon, she would be able to come into her garden again. And then, when everything had settled down, and if she felt comfortable, he'd be more than happy to take up her bins again on Tuesday nights.

Why he'd let things get so out of hand, he didn't know. He was just grateful for this moment of clarity and calm, as though the sun were warming him from the inside.

There was a small movement over the fence, and Malcolm's heart skipped a beat. Behind the sprawling westringia up against the fence between their houses, he could see the rounded softness of Mary's back as she knelt on her canvas cushion, her head bowed toward the ground. He took a step forward, straining to see more closely.

Mary's small hands, skin wrinkled and puckered like the setting point of jam, worked steadily in the soil. Her fingers were pinching out small green fronds: infant weeds, the slightest beginnings of weeds, weeds too little to know what they were themselves.

HOLD ME CLOSE

Edna watches a ladybug fumble across her knuckles and down to her dirt-encrusted fingernails. She holds still as it slips delicately onto a small rocket leaf next to her gardening boot. Yes, she thinks, tiny things have a knack of drawing your attention to bigger things. There are no ladybugs in Andrea's garden. No butterflies or bees. Andrea's garden – if Edna could even call it that – is static and lifeless. Andrea says that she and Gary don't have time for a garden. Andrea tells her – as if Edna is no longer a participant in it – that life is so much busier these days. Andrea says that there are plenty of parks within walking distance for Bertie and, one day, Violet to play in. 'Let the Council maintain them,' she says. 'That's why we pay rates,' she says. And Edna thinks, Codswallop! Is this Andrea talking, or Gary? For Edna has a theory about marriages: you think you know a person, when really you only know them as they are in relation to their spouse. Edna knows Andrea, of course. Edna believes she knows Andrea better than Gary does, possibly better than Andrea knows herself.

When Andrea was four years old, her best friend was Matty. Matty's family lived on the neighbouring property. At that age, the two would squirm back and forth through a small gap in the fence. Matty and Andrea told everyone that they were going to elope. No one knew where they got the word 'elope'. They spent their days making mud pies and catching blue tongue lizards for pets. Sometimes, at the end of a long day of play, Edna would throw them into the bath together and they would continue in their imaginary world, creating battleships from soap bars and lathering each other's hair into sculptures that they would give silly made-up names. Back then, Andrea used to say she wanted to be a truck driver like her father. Brian would fold his hands under his armpits, and his whole chest would shake as he chuckled, his stubborn waif of a daughter sitting up high in the cabin, her arms barely able to stretch the breadth of the steering wheel.

Now their daughter's life is all about antibacterial kitchen sprays and hair appointments and the right outfit for Gary's industry award nights.

Remembering that image of Brian laughing makes Edna smile and laugh out loud with a little snort through her nose.

Brian laughed a lot. Not the raucous, showy kind, but deep and constant like the undercurrent at Horseshoe Bay. There was always something funny when Brian was around. Even those last days in hospital, even then, Edna could see the dance of self-amusement in his eyes. Something always tickled Brian.

Edna nips out the weakest of the kale seedlings, smiling quietly to herself, when the telephone rings through the open kitchen window. She makes her way toward the house, but the machine clicks in before she gets there. Andrea and Gary set it to pick up after three rings, and Edna doubts an Olympic gymnast could make it before then. She resolves to unplug it. She'll give it to the Salvos.

Andrea's voice has the manic tone. 'Mum, it's Andrea. Are you there? Are you there, Mum? I hope everything's okay. Look, I'm wondering if you're coming into Mount Barker today. Look. Um ... just give me ...'

Edna reaches the phone but doesn't have time to catch her breath. 'I'm here.'

'Are you okay, Mum? You sound breathless.'

'Yes, darling, I'm fine.' Edna tries to control her breathing. Ever since the heart thing last year, her children have become like hawks, all three of them – watching, assessing, waiting to swoop. Take her to Sevenoaks Retirement Village. She's got one of these alert things she's supposed to wear around her neck too. If she presses the button a message will be sent to Andrea, Brendan and Jeremy. Apparently they will all call for an ambulance. Edna pictures three ambulances trundling down the long dirt driveway, lights flashing, dust billowing, bantams and big chooks squawking and flying off every which way. Some days she's tempted to press it, just to see that.

'Where were you?'

'In the garden.' Edna smiles but Andrea can't see that. 'Really, Andrea, I am fine. You're going to have to calm down about me. All of you.'

'We're all perfectly calm about you, Mum. Look, I'm sorry, I am. Things are falling apart for me a bit here. There's a party at eleven, and Michelle's been called in to sit with her mum who's got really sick again. Gary says he can't work from home – he's doing opens all day, apparently – so I don't know how I'm supposed to do this. I was wondering if you could come? Violet should sleep – I could take her with me, I suppose, but it's a hassle with all the stuff. Bertie could just watch TV, and you'd only have to do his lunch, but I can have that all ready. God, I don't know why I bother with it, actually. I'll probably only make fifty bucks, but you never know, that's the thing. You could get three more parties out of it. I cancelled on this woman last week already when Violet wasn't sleeping.'

Edna's breathing is back to normal, and she cuts in while she can. 'It's alright,' she tells her daughter. 'Relax. I can come directly. The ute's fixed now, and it's fine to drive. I'd like to come,' Edna says; 'I really would. It would be my pleasure' – she says that twice. Sometimes Edna feels as though Andrea can't hear her anymore, as though her voice is mute in Andrea's ears, as though her daughter's eyes don't see her properly.

Andrea does party plan sales for a scrapbooking company to supplement her half pay while she's on maternity leave. She tells her mother that it's a more flexible arrangement than going back to work early, and she explains that they need the extra little bit of money, to keep up the education fund. Edna privately rolls her eyes every time Andrea explains. When she thinks of what *they* survived on with three small children! If these kids were just a little bit more content with what is right in front of them. Normally, Andrea's friend Michelle babysits, and then Andrea reciprocates when Michelle does her parties. Because Michelle recruited Andrea, she gets a small cut from all Andrea's profits.

Every time Edna sees Michelle, she swears the girl has gained a few more pounds. Edna can't help but think of Michelle as profiting at her daughter's expense, as though Andrea is her golden goose.

When Edna thinks things like that – spiteful things about other people – Brian whispers in her ear. 'Let it be, love.' Or: 'Andrea's alright.' Brian is the most alive dead person Edna has ever known, the way he whispers in her ear like that. But all this talk of 'getting ahead' and 'profits'. It's not who Andrea is, it's not who *they* are, not who they've ever been.

Edna tells Andrea over and over that she's happy to look after her children because the truth is, Edna loves being with Bertie and gets a good feeling from Violet too. The baby girl has a presence – she keeps her steady eyes on Edna wherever she's in the room – and she's got a pair of lungs. Andrea (or maybe Gary?) says Edna shouldn't be left alone with the children. That she could have 'a turn'.

Though it seems today Andrea is desperate and her doubts about Edna are a low priority.

'What's "a turn" for goodness' sakes?' Edna says out loud. She does this more and more, especially when Brian is whispering. 'Who has "a turn"?' She looks about the cavernous kitchen of the homestead, dishes still piled from the day before, the floor smeared with dirt and leaf litter from her boots. She hears the swish of a light wind through the gums hanging over the shed and a few birds flitting around the garden outside the kitchen window.

~

She makes a concerted effort to scrub the dirt from her fingernails. She thinks about something to wear that her daughter will approve of. Not her gardening pants, or beekeeping overalls; not Brian's old *Say Yes to Refugees* t-shirt, the one she likes to wear in winter over a skivvy. The t-shirt is under her pillow these days. Some nights, she pulls it over her head in the dark, smooths it over her nightie, wraps her arms around herself.

She chooses the navy turtleneck jumper Andrea gave her a few years ago for Mother's Day. Dabs on a bit of lippy. It smells slightly rancid and feels dry on her mouth, and Edna muses that it's probably twenty years old. She looks at her face in Brian's little shaving mirror and believes she appears quite respectable.

She fills a basket with a dozen eggs and a bunch each of spinach, rocket and parsley, carefully washing and drying them first, even the eggs. No fruit to give – the oranges had a bad year, so Edna leaves them on the tree, will deal with them in marmalade later. Maybe she and Bertie will make a frittata today. She wishes they'd let him come and stay a night here. They never stay very long; never long enough for Bertie to get himself dirty and splash around in the puddles. When they come, Edna feels that Andrea and Gary look around the place as if they're doing a rent inspection. They hold themselves in a certain way, as if the surfaces might be sticky to touch.

Andrea and Gary live in an ex-display home village in Mount Barker, which is about fifteen minutes from the farm where Andrea grew up. Andrea says the only reason she still lives in Mount Barker is to keep an eye on Edna, otherwise they'd move to the city and Gary would sell apartments off the plan in Bowden. Edna knows that this is not true: Andrea has an excellent job at the Mount Barker hospital, the town is going mad with real estate work for Gary and, also, Andrea is not a city girl. How could she be, after the upbringing she had?

When Edna said that, Andrea raised her eyebrows and laughed, but not in a nice way. 'After the upbringing *I* had?' She shook her head back and forth for longer than Edna thought necessary.

Edna suspects Gary is quite controlling, that he feeds Andrea ideas about things he knows nothing about.

Mount Barker is a very different town from when Edna and Brian's children were young and they'd come through here as a family, in the truck. It was like a little country town back then, even with the milk factory and the tannery, though they're long closed. These days Edna thinks of it as a maddening jigsaw puzzle of shops and schools and houses. Every new shop seems to want to sell her a pizza. And all the silly estates with their big, God-awful houses and man-made lakes and ostentatious entrance gates. Edna can believe that someone like Mary Hillman would buy in an estate – that woman always thought she was better than everyone else – but her own daughter? 'This place isn't us,' she'd said to Andrea. 'Not *you*,' her daughter had snapped back, 'it's not *you*, Mum.' Brian would have understood; he'd have hated the big estates, but found them hilarious too. Edna sometimes tries to imagine the jokes Brain would make about things if he were still here. And then she tries to laugh at them, 'tries' being the operative word. Mostly, Edna avoids the town as much as she can, only comes in to see Bertie and Violet and collect her mail from the post office. She still drives Brian's old ute with the peacock they painted on the passenger door twenty years ago. Andrea says Edna sticks out like a sore thumb, and even Edna feels it. Andrea says it is only marginally better than when Edna used to ride the pushbike with the basket.

~

She

Edna parks the ute on the street so that Andrea can get her station wagon out. None of these houses have backyards. If Edna were forced to live here, she'd turn the front yard into a veggie patch. Andrea had scrunched her nose and winced at that, as if Edna had farted. 'Oh, Mum,' she'd said, 'that would look awful. Completely ruin the streetscape.'

Edna shakes her head, remembering her daughter saying 'streetscape'.

A path of white cement leads to the front door of Andrea and Gary's house. The path is lined with symmetrical bunches of thin, dark green strips: mature dwarf mondo grass. Beyond these the ground is covered in crushed granite. Under this, Edna believes her son-in-law has laid sheets of black plastic. Imagine covering living soil in plastic? It's like they've put a giant condom on their patch of earth – that's a Brian-style joke, and Edna smiles as she makes her way up the path. Dotted in and around the granite in seemingly random clusters (though, in fact, they're anything but) are plantings of one species of native grass, mid-green spiky straps. Tanika. It is a classic monocultural garden, rejected by mini-beasts and children alike.

Edna taps her special knock on Andrea's front door so that Bertie knows it's her. She hears his dimply three and a half-year-old fingers repeat it on the other side, and then she goes again while they both wait for Andrea to come and unlock the door. Edna can feel his little grin through the wood, and her skin starts to tingle in anticipation. She forces herself not to imagine Bertie in the ridiculous Prince Alfred College uniform Gary is so emphatic he will one day wear. The thought gives her a nasty shiver, because Bertie is something wondrous. He sprinkles joy around Edna's heart like the tiny blue wrens that hop around in her garden through the spring. She knows Brian would have loved him, and the knowledge is an ache.

As soon as the door opens, Edna sees Andrea's frazzled face before bobbing to Bertie's height. She slides her hand down the doorframe to keep balance. Bertie brings his fist up to Edna's face and spreads a warm, sticky hand across her nose and eyes. 'Gram Eddie,' he says, and the older woman breathes him in; he smells like orange peel and her own blue-gum honey. Bertie is a big fan of her honey, which pleases her, because it is full of nutrients. As Brian used to say, honey is the most underestimated and misunderstood wholefood there is.

Maybe she and Bertie will make honey crackles.

~

When Andrea finally leaves it is in a bustle of elbows and boxes and instructions. Violet is still asleep and Bertie is on the lounge-room floor playing with his wooden Thomas the Tank Engine set. His eyes have that mischievous grin in them that tells Edna he knows there'll be some fun once his mother leaves. Edna sneaks the boy one back as she nods to Andrea, who tells her that there's expressed milk in the fridge for Violet when she wakes, Bertie can have fish fingers, ABC3 has continuous kids' programs, and Edna has to ask Bertie every twenty minutes about the toilet. And don't go to the park, Andrea says. She won't be long, and it's too cold anyway. Fine, Edna thinks. She steps over Andrea's stack of wooden tissue-box holders – no doubt ready for her daughter's decoupage – and sits next to Bertie on the floor. She hears the click of the front door and then the sound of the ignition in the driveway.

Edna and Bertie build a circular farm with the wooden pieces and run the train through the middle. Edna watches her grandson's fingers manipulating the toys, his soft red lips pursing and flexing in concentration, his small feet tucked under his splayed knees, wrapped in the woollen socks she knitted for him. She focuses on their little world laid out on the carpet. It's an effort not to scoop him up and smother him with kisses, but it's also hard for her to sit so long on the floor, and after a while she tells the boy that Gram Eddie is going to make them lunch. He gives her a shy smile, nods up and down and then throws a wooden carriage across the floor where it hits the television screen.

'Oh no,' Edna says gently, 'the train stays on the tracks, Bertie.' And then she understands. 'Would you like to help

Gram Eddie cook lunch?' He looks up and widens his eyes and then jumps off the floor, ready for action – oh, to have a body as agile as that. Edna laughs and stands slowly in front of him, reaches back her arms and hooks his fingers around her thumbs. Edna chugs and *choo choos* a little breathlessly as they make their way into the kitchen with Bertie giggling and jogging behind. Edna trots a bit herself. She wishes they could all see her now. She is more than capable of entertaining a robust boy, thank you very much.

She carefully lifts Bertie and sits him on the kitchen bench while she fetches the fish fingers from the freezer. *Alaskan Pollock Fillets*, it says, crumbed in an orange concoction of E this and E that. Edna frowns, shakes her head in dismay.

Every summer holidays she and Brian would take their children to the Yorke Peninsula for four or five weeks on end. They'd stay in a local farmer's shack built out of corrugated iron and salvaged wood. No bathroom, no toilet, just a tap out back for washing the fish they caught and eventually themselves when their hair started to stand up from the saltwater. Brian used to transport the farmer's grain at harvest, and this little piece of paradise was part of the deal. They would spend the summer eating fresh King George whiting, dozens and dozens of tommy ruffs, snapper fillets, squid. The children swam, collected cockles for bait, explored the dunes, disappeared for hours and then reappeared salty and crusty and ravenous.

Edna clicks her tongue against her teeth. And yet here is Andrea, a grown woman and mother herself, buying these lurid rectangles to cook in this cappuccino-coloured kitchen of hers. It all looks and feels like cardboard – not only these fish fingers, but Andrea's whole house. Andrea is more interested in the look of things than the actual things themselves. Never mind that there's no insulation between their walls; Andrea is more concerned with what colour she'll paint them next. All through the house she has daubed little squares of colour from her test pots, all minute variations of beige that Edna can barely tell apart. What the house needs is insulation and wider eaves – a verandah, ideally.

'You sure you want these, buddy?' Edna screws up her nose.

Bertie laughs and nods, bangs his hands on the bench and sings, 'Ah-huh, ah-huh, ah-huh, ah-huh, ah-huh.'

'How many, then?'

He holds up three fingers, using his other hand to secure a renegade thumb.

'Oakley dokely,' Edna says, but she will suggest to Andrea that she consider buying Bertie fresh fish from the markets. She could crumb some bread herself, and it would be so much healthier. He's a growing boy! 'Now you stay there, mister,' she says to Bertie, and she taps him on the knee and looks into his eyes: they are the colour of hazelnuts. She turns her back, takes out three fish fingers and then puts the box back in the freezer. She can feel Bertie watching her as she moves slowly to the opposite side of the kitchen to switch on the stovetop. That's one thing that hasn't changed up here: no mains gas. She and Brian always used bottles at the farm, and she still does.

With a knob of butter and a little oil, the pan is soon sizzling. Once the fish fingers are in, Edna turns down the heat a bit so that they can thaw and cook through without burning. Of course, this would be easier with gas. While they cook, she holds her fingers up and dances them on her shoulder where Bertie can see. Facing the stove, she can't see him, but she can hear him chuckling and she knows that he won't move from the bench. When she turns, his face is lit up, his eyes filled with mirth. So like Brian this little one, more than any of the others.

'I see?' Bertie lifts the palm of one hand in a question, while the other stays clasping the side of the bench to keep his balance.

'Yes,' Edna says, and she moves closer to his side of the kitchen so that he can see her fingers dancing.

'Uh-uh. I see fingers in pan!' he says. 'Fishy fingers!'

'Oh, you want to see these funny things.' There is not enough space for Bertie to sit on the cooking side of the bench, and while Edna feels she could probably lift him, she knows he's too big to hold on her hip. 'When they're cooked, my cherub,' she tells him, 'then you can see.'

'No. I see them in the pan.'

So, Bertie wants to see the fish fingers cooking. And of course he does – the cooking is the interesting part, and he's a curious little chap. Well, then. Edna looks about. Such a nonsense kitchen; it looks nice and modern but is utterly impractical. What she needs right now is her own farm kitchen table, not this useless space between the two benches.

'You stay there,' she tells her grandson, 'and, in a minute, I'll bring this pan over so that you can have a good look at the fishy fingers frying.'

She flips the fingers and leaves them sizzling while she and Bertie sing 'Open Shut Them', and then she forages around

Andrea's cupboards for a trivet. If she sits the pan on the raised breakfast bar behind Bertie, he could turn around on the bench, kneel up and be able to see them inside. Andrea always helped her with cooking when she was small. The boys too. Edna would let them sit on the big kitchen table and crack eggs and stir cake mixtures and knead bread dough. Their noses and cheeks and hands covered in flour. Edna can picture it, as though it were yesterday.

She wonders if Andrea cooks with Bertie. Her pantry is filled with pre-made cake mixes and sachets of casserole bases. You would think she didn't know how to cook. Perhaps Gary does the shopping.

Edna pushes Andrea's stacks of craft paper to one side of the breakfast bar and then sits a wooden chopping board on top. She remembers that Andrea wanted this raised shelf specifically so that guests wouldn't see dirty dishes on the kitchen bench when they stood in the dining room. And yet, it's always covered in stuff.

'You wait there, my darling,' Edna tells Bertie. She turns the stovetop off and carries the fry pan over to Bertie's side. It is heavier than she thought and hard to lift up on to the breakfast bar over his head, but she manages and places it carefully down on the board. Bertie understands immediately and swivels around, clambering up onto his knees and then sitting back on his heels. Edna wonders if Andrea would ever let Bertie even sit on the kitchen bench. It was the biggest problem with parents today – mollycoddling. She moves her hands to either side of Bertie's thighs and holds them firmly, so that he can balance while he straightens up for a good look.

'There they are, Bertie. Fishies sizzling in the pan. Can you see?'

He nods. 'More?'

'Of course! Hands behind your back, first,' Edna says. She doesn't want Bertie to get overexcited and touch the pan with his soft little fingers. She hates the way people say 'don't' to inquisitive children, but she adds 'hot!' to be sure he understands. She tightens her hands so that he can sit up slightly higher without toppling.

With Edna's firm, weathered hands now wrapped around his calves, Bertie rises higher again. He cranes his neck down low to the pan, so that the rough, fried crumbs graze warm against the tip of his nose, and he pulls back low, too low. Too fast and too low. He takes a small, sharp breath in, and then a sound like the first wakeful cry of a baby.

Edna's flashing first thought is that the noise has come from Andrea and Gary's room where Violet is sleeping, but in the same instant Bertie throws his head back against her chest. He arches his neck hard, and Edna sees then that his eyes are filled with terror. He pulls both hands to his mouth and screams, 'Mouth! Mouth! Mouth!' He thrashes his body against hers, back and forth. She leans forward to regain balance, and her arm flies up and hits the chopping board, sending the fry pan off the breakfast bar and crashing to the floor on the other side. It is not until Edna has sunk to the floor with Bertie screaming in her lap that she fully comprehends that he has burnt his mouth against the side of the fry pan. She knows she needs to get cold water, but she can't lift him while he is thrashing against her like this. Her legs feel strangely numb and tangled, and her chest is thumping painfully. She knows she must act quickly, but some crucial, necessary part of her is sinking somewhere else, somewhere slow and curdled. Brian. Oh, Brian.

She tries to find her voice. When it comes, it is cracked and uncertain. 'It's okay, Bertie. Gram Eddie is here. It's okay, Bertie. We'll fix it, we'll fix it.'

But Bertie can't hear her over his screams. She can barely hear herself. Finally, she lets go of him and manages to stand up. She reaches the sink, wrings the dishcloth in cold water. She kneels back down and presses the cloth to his mouth. She can see that it is blistering fast, across his lip and down one side of his chin. His face is blotched red all over, his pupils huge. She holds him in her lap until his sobs turn into hiccups, and he falls limp and exhausted against her knees. She realises then that he has wet his pants, remembers she was supposed to ask him about the toilet. And Violet has woken and is crying from another room.

~

When Andrea gets back, Bertie is asleep in his bedroom, and Edna is sitting on the lounge nursing Violet with the bottle. Andrea is loaded up again with boxes and bags of samples, but she looks flushed and satisfied with herself. She puts her things down and smiles at Violet and Edna. 'Where's Bertie?'

'Darling, he's asleep.'

Andrea frowns and angles her head. 'Bertie hasn't had a day sleep in over a year,' she says. She is still, squinting at her mother.

'We had a bit of an accident,' Edna says slowly. 'He's okay. It's just a little burn. I'm sorry he hasn't had any lunch, though.'

Andrea stares at Edna for another moment, and then drops her last bag and walks out of the lounge. Violet finishes the bottle, and Edna sits her up and cradles her chin between thumb and index finger to burp her.

When she returns, Andrea is holding Bertie in her arms like a baby. He is awake and watching her with big eyes, wet and red from crying and disoriented from sleeping. Andrea glances from him to Edna and back. 'Jesus, Mum.'

Edna can't bring herself to look directly at Bertie's lip, but it is obvious, even from where she sits, that it is puffed and swollen.

'Why didn't you call me?' Andrea squats down and fumbles to pick her handbag up again. When she stands, she looks at Edna and then at Violet on her lap and then to either side of her, as if she has lost something. Her lips are moving as if she is having an urgent conversation with herself. 'He needs to go to the doctor, Mum.' She says this firmly. 'Did you think about him going into shock?' She says it as though Edna is the last sheep left in the pen that might try and jump. Edna gets the trilling thing in her chest that feels like choking but isn't.

Andrea shakes her head back and forth. Then she asks her mother to follow her outside and to put Violet in her capsule. Edna brings Violet to her chest and holds her there as she follows Andrea out to the car. Their eyes meet briefly as Andrea straps Bertie in his toddler seat on the other side of the car. Andrea makes cooing sounds and strokes his hair. Then she comes around to Edna's side and checks that Violet's straps have been done up properly.

Edna reaches to open the door handle on the front passenger side, but Andrea puts a hand on her shoulder.

'It's okay,' she says. 'You go home. I'm going straight to the hospital. One of the GPs will be on. I'll call you.'

~

The phone doesn't ring until 10pm, but when it does, Edna picks up on the first ring. There is a scratching sound, and at first she can't hear properly, but then she realises her daughter has her hand over the mouthpiece and she is saying something to a man who is in the background; Edna realises it is Gary talking, and there are other sounds too, and she assumes that Violet has just woken. She pictures Gary lifting Violet out of the cot, and she imagines that the two of them are discussing whether Andrea should feed the baby or not. Edna imagines this whole picture, and she stays quiet on her end until Andrea is ready to speak to her.

Andrea's voice is weary and she sounds a long way away. 'It will heal,' she says finally, 'but he'll have a scar. Right under his lip.' Edna thinks Andrea might be crying softly. 'He's not even four,' she says, 'and he's already going to have a scar.'

~

Edna can't think what to do when she's hung up the phone. She knows that she won't sleep. She knows that there is little point in even going to bed. She knows that Bertie will be okay, that a tiny scar isn't the end of the world. But every time she tries to settle, she sees Bertie's face in her mind's eye, and she feels as though a huge tidal wave is about to engulf her and she won't be able to breathe.

The farm house feels big, too big. It is cold, and she wanders around it a little aimlessly trying to think of a task that might settle her. Normally, she makes soup tonight to last for the week, but she doesn't. She can't bring herself to light the fire either, but she sits in the old armchair in front of it anyway and pulls her cross-stitch from the basket on the floor. It is a posy of violets, she had thought perhaps for Violet's bedroom. She can hear the wind whistling outside through the gum trees and the beginning of rain on the roof. She focuses on her hands pushing the needle down into the cloth, and she sees that her hands are shaking. They seem foreign to her, bony and mottled with strange brown spots. She doesn't recognise her own hands. She realises that her jaw is shivering too, and she presses her teeth together. She drops the cross-stitch back into the basket and clasps her hands in her lap. She is an old woman sitting alone in a house that is cold and too big for her.

Edna closes her eyes and begins to shake all over, unravelling like crinkled woollen thread.

'Hush,' he whispers.

She folds her arms around herself and cranes forward in her husband's armchair.

'Hush, my love.'

THE FOURTH DIMENSION

The town of Mount Barker has the sort of people who use the phrase 'salt of the earth'. That's how they'd describe Bob Lang. They'd call him 'a good bloke'. Frances hasn't actually heard any of this, but she senses it, in the same way you instinctively know when a child is loved and not merely clothed and fed. But after she has driven the length of Huon Close, circled the cul-de-sac and nosed her Yaris into her yet-to-be-paved driveway, she will no longer share this view of the local builder. Frances will see the wooden thing sticking up from the tip of her roof. The finial.

In front of her, his back turned, Bob angles tools into a wheelbarrow. The man, his tools and his wheelbarrow are lightly coated in the fatigued patina of dust and dried cement, layer upon layer, accumulated over years together in the building industry.

Frances sits in her Yaris at the top of the driveway, ensconced in cream faux-leather upholstery, and casts her eyes upward from Bob to the apex of the roof.

Yes, the finial is still there. Her eyes narrow. Her heart picks up speed. In a back recess of her mind she hears music and thinks of tempo: *accelerando* and also *più mosso*. Phantom ants march up her neck and sting into her hairline. She gets out of the car, threads her arm through the handle of her handbag and tucks it under an elbow. Smooths her hands down the sides of her small but shapely thighs, down her navy crepe pants from Jacqui E. Her pelvis thrusts forward as she navigates the stupidly steep driveway. She steels herself from the mental image of her beloved baby grand being winched down this slope on moving day. She reminds herself: flat blocks were much too expensive.

She'd discussed the finial with Bob on Tuesday. It was her one and only – her only – modification to the Cab Sav courtyard home. No finial, like the Sorrento, except it's the Cab Sav. Stipulated in her contract. Straightforward. Bob nodded several times but said that in his opinion the Cab Sav looked better with the finial. He said the Cab Sav was *designed* to have the finial. Frances was surprised that Bob had such a strong opinion; he was just the builder, for God's sake. 'That may well be,' Frances said, 'but I don't want the finial, so it needs to be left off, whatever it takes.' He nodded again. He said, 'Right,' which Frances naturally took to mean, 'Right, I'll do it.'

People usually made much more demanding modifications, and Frances knew it. If she'd chosen the simpler Sorrento, she'd have had to change the whole lounge/dining/kitchen configuration to achieve her piano wall. It wasn't only about avoiding the drafts. If you opened the lid toward the right wall, you got to hear the big sound directly from the piano stool, and that's what she wanted. In the new piano room, she could do away with monitoring water levels on the humidifier. Probably she'd no longer need one. In this room, she was having hardwood floorboards installed to enhance the subtle, mellow voice of her Kawai.

Surely it was easier to build the Cab Sav sans finial?

~

'Bob.'

He turns and crosses his arms over his broad, squat chest, stretching to tuck his fingertips under his armpits. Frances thinks of footballers' photographs.

He lifts his eyebrows.

'Bob. The finial. It's still there.' Frances points to the roof, wobbles slightly as the small heel of her court shoe slips across a large piece of gravel. Later, she will find a gash in the patent leather. Her eyes shift to the waiting pallet of sandstone pavers, and she feels a rush of impatience akin to the sensation of a bucket of tepid water poured over her head.

'Uh-huh.' Bob turns to pick up the handles of the wheelbarrow.

'Right.' Her eyes widen. 'Okay.' She drawls the 'okay' sideways, wondering what approach to take, even though she knows that Bob isn't listening. She thinks, *Ad libitum*. She must be diplomatic. Stay on his good side.

She remembers the conversation with Warwick and the other doctors and their partners the night before.

'You don't want to piss off your builder,' Warwick said. 'You absolutely need to stay on his good side.'

'Hear, hear,' said Tim. His wife Louise lifted her glass in agreement, pursed her lips into a small smile toward Frances and took a sip. Brenton said, 'Absolutely,' and Cassie, his new partner, a blonde agency nurse, murmured, 'Absolutely,' right on its heels. Brenton: 'For God's sake, make him a batch of your raspberry and white chocolate muffins.' Laughing and more wine. Warwick draped his arm around Frances's chair and stroked his fingertips back and forth across the round of her shoulder. Irritating, but she laughed with the others.

Tim asked what she had against finials. 'She thinks they're daggy – architecturally inappropriate,' Warwick answered. 'She wants her house to be *honest* – architecturally honest.' When he said 'architecturally', he spelt out all the separate sounds of the word as though he were riding it like a rollercoaster. He squeezed Frances's shoulder, pulling her into his armpit. She smiled and shrugged, shook her head to try and free the hairs that had become caught under Warwick's jacket and were pulling against her scalp.

Tim: 'Hey! Maybe this is the *fourth dimension* – you know.' He intimated quotation marks around his ears when he said 'fourth dimension'. 'You know – emotion in architecture? Like the finial is bringing up something from your childhood.' Smiles and silence. Tim again: 'Aren't they supposed to deter witches on broomsticks from landing on your roof, finials? Sure you don't want one, Frances?' More laughing.

She already knew this. She'd looked it up on Wikipedia at work. The doctors had recently paid for a new reception desk, and the configuration of desk, return, computer and switchboard meant that she could now look at her screen without patients seeing it as well – a definite improvement. Yes, she'd thought. Finals are for fairytales.

'Look,' she said to the amused dinner table assembly, 'it's really no big deal. Nothing from my childhood or a former life. I just don't want it. And yes, I think they're daggy. They're so – I don't know – *try-hard*. Fake. But, you know, I don't really have such a big opinion on it. Not really.'

Warwick raised his eyebrows, smiled and leant down to kiss the top of her head. The others continued watching. Warwick took his arm away and shifted low in his chair, stretching his long, bowed legs into a human slide under the table. The two women smiled at Frances with the patience of colluding schoolgirls.

'It's just one thing I happened to change on the design,' Frances went on. 'You can basically change whatever you want.' She looked around the table. 'You've all built houses, you know how it works – people change whole rooms around! Laundry here. Bathroom there. All I don't want is one of those ridiculous finials on my roof.'

What did she want? She couldn't even articulate it. Every time she tried, it sounded too silly in her brain to send it down to her mouth.

The three men grinned, and she remembered that the houses they had built were originals, designed by architects, every aspect to their specification. Warwick had built his after the divorce, using the same architect as Tim and Louise. He wanted Frances to live with him. He'd said, 'You know you're more than welcome to just move in here with me.' Brenton and Cassie were renting in the city, in the interim, while Brenton's wife stayed in their five-bedroom, split-level house with their kids. Frances hadn't seen Karen since the split. It dawned on her only then that Karen, with whom she had got along quite well, had shared dinners and bottles of wine and cups of coffee, even the odd weekend away, was no longer part of her life.

~

Maybe it's not even the finial, Frances thinks now. Bob has turned his back on her and is wheeling his load of tools around to the back of the house. She follows him in a half-trot. The cuffs of her pants skim and collect pigeon lime. Maybe it's some symbolic phallic thing. Maybe she has a problem with men. Maybe this is why she hasn't married, why none of her relationships have lasted more than two years. She's thirty-five, for God's sake. Maybe she needs counselling.

No; it is a simple matter of aesthetics. And they are *her* aesthetics.

And it might be tacky, but it's true – she just hasn't found 'the one'. She isn't afraid to say it: she wants more than a friendship, a partnership, some kind of business arrangement. She wants *passion*. She can't describe what she wants with words, but she *feels* it whenever she plays herself Tchaikovsky. And then she finds herself sitting on the piano stool and wondering how she came to be a 35-year-old single medical receptionist living in Mount Barker and building in

Gladeview Park estate.

Anyway, she isn't entirely single. There is Warwick. Warwick and the finial, she thinks. How ridiculous.

~

Her arm scrapes against brick as she takes the corner of her new house too quickly, pilling her cream blouse. She checks her watch. 12.15. A half-hour lunchbreak barely gives you time to buy something to eat.

'Ah, excuse me. Bob?'

Bob continues walking until he reaches the back of the house and sets down the wheelbarrow. He turns to face her, resuming the footballers' photograph pose. He has leathery skin from a lifetime under the Australian sun, creviced, creased and mottled with shadows. Thin strips of grey and black hair sweep across his scalp. Sideburns like unused balls of steel wool. Hard to pick, but Frances guesses early fifties. She tries to imagine that a woman might find him attractive. He lifts his stubbled chin at her in a quick motion, which Frances reads as: *Speak*.

She takes a small step backward. 'Look. Maybe you haven't got to it yet, but ... well, I'm just checking on the finial. Look, everything else is fine. It's fine.' She gestures with her hand; up, down and around. 'But, I'd like to know when you are going to remove the finial, please.' She thinks of Warwick with the 'please'.

Bob squints his eyes, sharpens his mouth into a point and takes it to one side, drops his head further into his neck.

Frances's right foot involuntarily rises an inch and stamps

back down. She steadies the palms of her hands onto her thighs. 'Look. Bob. I have a stipulation in my contract.' She already went through this on Tuesday, but she does it again, this time more slowly, a conscious effort at light-heartedness. She finishes her monologue and asks Bob to give her a clear indication of when the finial will be removed. She lifts her chin and adds, 'Please.'

'Won't look right.' Bob shakes his head back and forth, like a toddler shoring up for a tantrum. 'The Cab Sav needs the finial. It's part of the *design*.' He emphasises the 'd' and rocks forward onto his toes and then back down to his heels.

Frances stares about her for sympathy from an equally bewildered but imaginary audience. She says his name as if she's trying to pounce on it. 'Listen. It doesn't matter if it's part of the design or not. The thing is, I'm changing it. And if it doesn't look right, then it's my fault. Because it's ... it's, well, it's actually my house. Okay?'

'No.'

'No, what?' She takes a step toward him, exhales sharply. *Staccato*: 'Do you not agree that this is my house?'

'I won't change it. Won't look right. Look, yer chose the Cab Sav, so obviously yer like the *style* of the house. The finial is part of the style. Yer would've been more than welcome to change the interior around. But yer can't change the *integrity* of the *style*.' He pauses, lifts and narrows his eyes with the look of a person who has just solved the final clue to a deep mystery. His voice drops, softer – 'No one has ever wanted me to leave off the finial. Everyone wants the finial. It's part of the Cab Sav. Yer don't *want* the Cab Sav without the finial.'

'But I do want the Cab Sav, because I've got it!' Frances throws an arm skyward. Gravity flops it heavily back down. Her heart gallops into her throat. She speaks through her teeth, jaw clamped and eyes stinging. 'And you have to take it off because I don't want it. I don't want the finial! And I'm paying for this house, and you are the builder who is getting my money. So, take the finial off now! Please!'

Later, she will sit in the new IKEA armchair in her rented unit, dabbing Dettol and cotton wool at the cuts on her hands, wincing, mentally rephrasing these last words until they sing, until they are compelling enough, she imagines, to be delivered in a film or printed in a book. She will also kick her shoes off and notice the slash down the leather of one heel.

Bob rubs his chin, turns and picks up the wheelbarrow. Starts to walk away from her.

'Excuse me!' Frances's voice cracks. 'I ... I ... well, I'm going to have to call your boss. This is outrageous. You are so completely ...' Adjectives and insults tumble and vie for her selection, but she can't settle on one that is up to the task. She fumbles in her bag for her phone. She holds it in her hand, which she sees is shaking. She wonders about calling Warwick first, whether he might come down and talk to Bob. That man-to-man thing. She exhales sharply. This is meant to be her house. It would not only be humiliating to call Warwick, it would also be pathetic. She's sure the number is in her phone. She steadies her thumb to scroll down her contacts. Sees Karen. She liked Karen. They got along well. Perhaps she needs a friend to give her some perspective, some on-the-spot advice.

A phone rings, but it's not the one she's holding. A loud, old-fashioned ring. Bob fumbles into the bib pocket of his khaki overalls stretched tight across his large, barrelled ribcage. He pulls out a thick black phone encased in a baggy pouch. He holds it first in front of his face and then extends his arm fully and leans his head back, squinting at it. The continuing ring is so obtrusive that Frances is compelled to pause from her own task, like someone might if a freight train were passing.

'Bob.' He grunts his name into the phone, but then his face softens. 'Son. Yes, son.' He nods quietly. 'You were there? Mish?' Nods again. 'Okay. Right then. Right then. I didn't think it would be today. Right then. I'll see you directly.'

Bob walks to the back wall of Frances's house and places a palm against the bricks. It took her a whole month to choose the russet of Old Red Sandstock over Sapphire. Bob drops his head for a moment, and Frances wonders if his lips might be moving.

He turns his chin up over his arm and says, 'Have to go.'

'Pardon?' Frances grips her phone more tightly. She folds her arms across her stomach and watches as Bob leans over his wheelbarrow. He rearranges the wood and steel handles of the larger tools until he is satisfied with their symmetry and order, and then he picks out the big, dented metal toolbox from the bottom of the tray. It looks to have once been painted blue; chips and patches of colour remain on the top and sides. Frances imagines the toolbox in a trendy shabby-chic shop in the city. She watches as Bob takes the toolbox and turns his back to angle past her. She would move, but she seems to be stuck there.

As Bob turns the corner of the house, she hears herself screech his name again. 'Bob! Bob! Excuse me! Where are you going?'

Bob stops, turns slowly back and, for a moment, is perfectly still. Frances watches him closely. Grey dust freckles his head and face, making him look as though he is made of stone. She sees a small black mole underneath his left eye and notices too that his eyes are a soft green.

'There you are, then,' he says finally. 'She's dead.'

'What?'

'My wife. She's dead.'

'Oh.'

'Cancer.'

'Oh. I'm ... well ... I'm sorry.'

Bob lifts the toolbox slightly higher. 'Don't be sorry.' Then he looks over her head and raises his voice, as if addressing a whole group of people, and says, 'Forty years next Saturday.' To himself, he mutters it again, 'Forty years.' And then he turns and walks away.

Frances places her hands and face against the glass of her dining-room window. Through the empty shell of her house, she catches a glimpse of Bob in the lounge window as he makes his way up the driveway, toolbox in hand. The steepness exposes a drooped shoulder she hadn't noticed before – as though he were nursing a broken collarbone. She crouches and sees his boots as they step up into his old white ute. She hears the engine start and the sound of the tyres as they spin briefly on gravel and dust and then clunk down the kerb from her yet-to-be-landscaped front yard. The monstrous river red gum at the top of her block is unfazed and majestic as Bob's ute disappears over the rise of Huon Close. No one wanted the possibility of falling limbs, and Frances knew the so-called significant tree was another reason her lot was so affordable. She tries not to think about it.

After a moment, Frances stands and walks the short distance to Bob's abandoned wheelbarrow. Gazing into the tools, something emerges in her throat, something more she might like to say to Bob, as if part of him is still here, somehow part of the tools – as if they are his extended limbs. She opens her mouth, but it is a strange groan that forms, not a word or even the notion of a word. A bird lands on the steel guttering above her, its tiny feet tapping like keyboard keys, and she thinks vaguely of her reception desk at work. She lifts a hand and touches one of the long wooden handles. Old grey oak. Her fingers run along the length of it, and she marvels at how silky and smooth it is – and warm – like running her hand down the trunk of a ghost gum in summer when she was a girl. She feels pleased to have timed the building of her house outside the winter months with all the rain and mud; she'd seen how messy that could get on her walks through the estate last year. She reminds herself: she does have some control of things. Her fingers reach a cold steel blade, which she assumes is an axe. Her fingers drop to the next tool, a shorter iron rod topped with a sharp steel rectangle.

What Frances does next is difficult for her to recall later, perhaps because her actions carry no accompanying thoughts. There are no words, no interior commentary, as she separates and lifts this last tool away from the others, feels the weight of it across her shoulderblade, and makes her way to the front of her house. At no point does she think, I'll do it myself. Nor does she think, I'll find a ladder.

When she has accomplished this thought-free action, having stumbled once on a steel rung, ripped a small hole where her pant pocket meets the leg seam, and cut her left hand badly enough that it will eventually receive three stitches, Frances lugs herself and her handbag up the driveway and sits down in the dust, resting against the front right tyre of her Yaris; it does not occur to her to sit in the car. Her eyes travel from the ground where the severed finial lies alongside the wrecking bar, up past the bricks and gutter to the tip of the roof, where the splintered base remains. A small measure of peace arrives in her chest, unforeseen and fleeting but leaving its trace, like a stranger with a kindly voice who has rung the wrong number. It is not the peace Frances had hoped for, but it is still peace.

She thinks absentmindedly that this must be the longest lunchbreak she has ever taken in her life. An image of her unattended desk floats briefly across her mind, the new Béla Bartók screen saver no doubt scrolling across her computer. She knows her absence will confound Warwick, as will the image of Bartók, for while he thinks he knows everything, he is so ignorant of her music. She closes her eyes, tilts her head to rest against the side of her car, the warmth of the sun and the hard ground beneath her.

Brightling.

THE FIVE TRUTHS OF MANHOOD

1. You are going to die

Malcolm has every reason to believe that he'll be fine. The word 'fine' laps gently in his mind like the outgoing tide on a sheltered bay. From resting heartbeat to penile erection, Malcolm's wiry 49-year-old body has never given him cause to complain. Things Malcolm can't see too, those that slide around in darkness, have always done so, smooth and effortless. And while his temperament is inclined to melancholy and rumination, not once has this made its way into any *public* realm – certainly it has never required professional intervention. Malcolm has always been functional. He notices the full-page Breitling Navitimer watch advertisement featuring John Travolta and finds it strangely reassuring. The magazine sits on the colonial coffee table wedged to the right of Malcolm's chrome chair in the Wellington Road Medical Surgery. He picks it up, crosses a knee and rests the magazine on his thigh.

Taking up most of the page with his sure frame, Travolta sits on the ground with his back resting against a retro aircraft. His denim-clad knees are bent, his posture casual, but in his eyes there is a gaze of conviction. A sliver of his Breitling Navitimer watch creeps past the sleeve edge of his bomber jacket. Aviation enthusiasts like Travolta – most people were only acquainted with the star, the multifaceted actor – trusted their Breitling watch for its standards of precision, sturdiness and functionality. Equipped with movements, Malcolm reads, that are chronometer-certified by the COSC. Malcolm stares at the advertisement and feels a surge of boyhood camaraderie and then a sting of envy. The feeling itself is familiar, but also vague and disorienting, like seeing yourself in an old photograph on an occasion you don't remember.

Malcolm averts his eyes to his own watch, flimsy and cheap by comparison. It is just past two and something is awry. There is no one behind the reception desk here for starters, and the waiting room is full. An overweight boy in a grey school shirt sits slumped next to him groaning, red cheeked, sweating, and on the verge, Malcolm assesses, of vomiting. Malcolm feels no anxiety about the child being potentially contagious, although others might. He realises the boy is probably of a similar age to his own son, who can appear younger than he is on account of being rake thin.

Malcolm himself isn't handsome; he knows that. Thin, slightly ungainly, a nose that makes delicate reference to a flower bulb. But Malcolm's lack of sex appeal has not hindered his success in life. He is no film star, no aviator, sure. But he has an MBA and is an established and (he is quite certain) respected manager in the hospital's Technology Acquisition Unit. And he's making decent inroads on a mortgage that is well below the national average, giving him over 75 per cent equity in what could only be described as an enviable home and garden: new, spacious, high quality, 9-foot ceilings, landscaped, with a view. Not least of all, he has Theresa, has her as his wife and the mother of his son, who, apart from a number of setbacks entirely out of the boy's control, is doing okay, is doing quite well. All things considered.

Malcolm doesn't like sitting around waiting, doing nothing on a day when he would normally be at work. After the follow-up tests on Monday, this is the second day in the same week that Malcolm has had off work. Two days and two lies; on both Malcolm had dressed for work and left at his normal time. He did not want to worry his wife or his son.

The fact that he has never had a day off work for sickness before is not because he is stoic. Malcolm simply doesn't get sick. The initial appointment almost two weeks ago was a yearly ritual Malcolm had begun to privately enjoy since he'd turned forty-five and Theresa had made him take advantage of the government-funded Healthy Man Health Check. Theresa's own father had died a slow and painful death at fifty that could have been prevented, she said, if he'd just gone to a bloody doctor once in his life. That's the last thing Martin needs, she said; to lose his father. And even though she was criticising him for being un-self-aware and delusional like her father, he'd felt warmed to hear his wife say that losing him was the *last* thing their son needed. He'd humoured her with the first major overhaul, not anticipating the pleasant feeling he would have watching the young GP nod with approval as he ran down the pathology report. And on top of that, a BMI of 20, blood pressure 120/80, not a single mole or freckle to declare and yes thanks, he did feel 'on top of things' – at work and at home? Yes. Thank you.

Every year since it had been the same, not a single aberration. Commendable, said Dr Rossiter the second year. No need to come back until you're fifty, he said the third year, and when he did come back anyway, Dr Rossiter scanned his bloods and said: 'Uncanny.'

~

'Malcolm Wheeler?'

Not Dr Rossiter today. Instead, it is the unfamiliar and bow-legged Dr Mitchell.

Malcolm stands and follows him down the cream-coloured passage until he stops outside Room 3. He motions for Malcolm to enter. The doctor is taller than Malcolm and with a largeness and gait that speak of the eastern seaboard, private schools and rugby games. He sits in his own chair, squares his body and gestures with an index finger toward one of the empty visitor's chairs. The room smells of antibacterial hand wash combined with yeast, and Malcolm remembers that he didn't eat lunch; the chicken and avocado sandwich he'd made for himself must still be sitting on the kitchen bench. He'd made the mistake of flicking on the flat screen, curious about the daytime soap that the women in Supply always gossiped about: *Days of Our Lives*. They recorded it every day and then watched it at night. If Malcolm had made the more logical decision of taking the sandwich *with* him to the rumpus room, his stomach wouldn't be rumbling now. Or if he'd known how long he was going to have to wait, he could have comfortably stayed home another ten minutes and eaten the sandwich then. Or, he could have eaten it in the car. So many small regrets.

He considers the temperature (27 according to the *Advertiser*, minus one or two to accommodate the latitude of the hills), the amount of time the sandwich has already sat unrefrigerated (one and a half hours) and he begins to formulate what he will Google when he gets home (*How long can chicken stay out at 25 degrees Celsius?* say, or maybe, *How long chicken unrefrigerated?*). Malcolm has begun to feel a measure of pride in his increasing ability to acquire specific information through Google. Even his twelve-year-old son occasionally would defer to Malcolm's skills when it came to school projects. Given the boy's obsession with computers (in part contributing to his so-called Asperger's diagnosis), Malcolm considered Martin's requests not just an opportunity for bonding, but a very real compliment.

Malcolm watches Dr Mitchell draw his finger back and forth across his bottom lip, scratch with it behind his ear and then run it down the page inside Malcolm's open patient file. Then the doctor looks up, and while his face is empty and non-committal, these words come out of his mouth:

'Significant', 'afraid', 'shock', 'unfortunately', 'bowel cancer' and 'possible metastasis'.

Malcolm chuckles politely. Smiling, he says, 'No,' as if Dr Mitchell has made a small and indiscreet joke. 'I feel absolutely fine. Never felt better, actually.' But then Malcolm quickly understands that this is irrelevant – people with cancer diagnoses often feel fine, certainly could look fine, he knew that. And so: 'There must be some kind of mistake,' he says, 'some kind of pathology *mix-up*.'

Dr Mitchell smiles patiently. He swivels his chair from his desk, plants his feet a good distance apart from one another and rests his forearms casually on his knees. Like John Travolta in front of the plane, thinks Malcolm. This is no joke.

Malcolm notices then that Dr Mitchell – 'please, call me "Warwick"' – is wearing the same navy socks with the bright blue thin vertical lines that he himself is wearing. This strikes Malcolm as ironic, although he's not sure how.

The plastic clock on the wall ticks with a slow and painful effect, as though every second hurts it.

Malcolm doesn't want to call him Warwick. Too close, too sentimental.

He steadies himself as he signs the Medicare form at the front desk, unsure whether Dr Mitchell bulk bills him out of compassion (and perhaps the anticipation of many consults ahead) or whether he doesn't know how to use the EFTPOS machine in the absence of a receptionist.

2. Life is hard

In the carpark, Malcolm sits for several minutes in his Subaru wondering what he should do – not in terms of decisions (yes, Dr Mitchell had mentioned decisions) or even preparations, he can't fathom how many of those he must make – but right now. Is this when he should ring his wife? Tell her, *I've got cancer*? He checks his watch. School will be over in twenty minutes and then Theresa will be heading to a staff meeting, then Wednesday Wine and Cheese. (It was a far cry from the stale Milk Arrowroots they'd got at her old school.) Then she'll probably go to Curves, before picking Martin up from OSHC. He feels himself slipping, and he sits up higher in his seat, puts his hands on the steering wheel.

The wheel is almost too hot to touch, even though it's not yet summer – presumably evidence of global warming. This makes Malcolm think of the solar panels on their roof at home, so far having made no difference at all to their electricity bill. He wraps his fingers tightly around the black plastic until his knuckles go white and his eyes sting. Unbidden random phrases in thick American accents appear in his mind from *Days of Our Lives:*

> *I'm really sorry about your loss, honey.*
> *But deep down, doesn't it feel ... kinda neat?*
> *That doesn't really help right now. I just feel so empty.*

The woman had lost a baby. Now she was pregnant again and close, in today's episode, to giving birth. She had been sprayed, Malcolm guessed, with a fine mist of water to look like perspiration, and she huffed and puffed when her fictitious contractions came. When the women in Supply discussed '*Days*', as they called it, gasping and laughing and saying 'I know!' they sometimes joked that you could miss a year's worth of episodes but still know what was happening. Malcolm wasn't so sure.

There's so much *draaaaaaama*, the Supply women would say, and they always stretched the word out like that.

The obvious thing would be to call Theresa, or his sister – or even his work. Would he go to work tomorrow? He would need to see Dr Rossiter, go over the whole thing again, properly. He squints his eyes against the sun and starts the engine.

For now, the inscrutable fact that Malcolm allegedly has potentially inoperable bowel cancer exists only in a manila folder and in the walls of a small uninspired room that smells of hand sanitiser and something else that he can now pinpoint: Subway.

'Potentially inoperable' are not words that Malcolm has dramatically conjured. Dr Mitchell used them. Malcolm doesn't want to ring anybody, doesn't want to talk to anybody, not even Theresa, especially not his sister and definitely not work. What he wants is to be wrapped in darkness. To be coaxed into oblivion. Suspended, somehow. Relieved, at the very least, from this ferocious daylight.

3. You are not in control of the outcome

Only once has Malcolm ever been to the movies during the day, and that too was under exceptional circumstances. It feels odd but it is the only place he can think of and he marvels at his ability to have brought himself here. He is the only one in the cinema. He settles his lemonade into the plastic holder at the end of the armrest and nestles the medium-sized popcorn between his knees.

There had been blood, like they say in the pamphlets. He wasn't stupid. He'd just assumed that it was something else, something simple. A fissure or a haemorrhoid, whatever – either would have been significant enough in the context of his medical history. It was all documented now in his patient file.

Malcolm feels a sudden grief for the manila folder itself, for the weight it now carries, its new stigma and loss of anything to commend or call uncanny. *His* name bearing down its spine. Malcolm Wheeler, in capitals. *His* undesirable facts inside: the bloods, the colonoscopy and the biopsy and soon, he imagines, CT scan, surgery notes and some ill-conceived medication regime: 5-FU, probably Oxaliplatin – he's not naive about this stuff. He imagines his file tucked a quarter of the way across the W's in that large steel compactus – no doubt a Dexion Mekdrive, manufactured right here in his home state.

He's come in late, missed the Val Morgan advertising, a relief of sorts. Some forgettable chick flick with that actor who married Demi Moore. What was wrong with Bruce Willis? It strikes Malcolm that any film he sees today, even this stupid one, will be significant. That he will remember it, with everything else.

Because he is going to die. *He is going to die.* It reverberates through his brain until he can focus on nothing else. And then suddenly everything speaks of it – everything – the drapes of floor-to-ceiling fabric hanging down the walls, each flicker of movement on the screen, the most elementary laws of physics holding his drink in its cup and his shoes on the floor. Even the palm-oil infused popcorn disintegrating on Malcolm's tongue speaks the truth of his impending death. *You are going to die.* This comes to Malcolm as though it is spoken aloud and amplified across the cinema. It was the first of the 'five truths of manhood'. Theresa had just given him Biddulph's latest book. He skim read it to make her happy when they rented that shack on the river, but he hadn't really taken it in. There were five truths of manhood, according to some Franciscan monk, and Biddulph was big on it. What were the other four truths? He counts on his fingers in the dark: one, *you are going to die;* two, *it's not about you;* no that's three, something about not being in control and not being important. He can't remember. He feels his chest crumple. He presses a thumb and forefinger onto the bridge of his nose, pressing down into the corners of his eyes. And then he is washed in a memory, of the only other time he was in a cinema during the day.

Wonder Boys: not particularly interesting or good, but it was twelve years ago last Saturday that Malcolm and Theresa had gone to the cinema and like today, bought tickets to whatever was on. When Theresa had stood up as the credits rolled down, pushing awkwardly on Malcolm's knee for leverage, her waters had broken. Spectacularly and dramatically, just like in the movies, they would joke. They'd left the mess and driven straight to the Women's and Children's hospital. The night Martin was born. It was a blur; Malcolm couldn't think and then he could, Martin was blue and then he was pink and Theresa cried and then she laughed. And the whole room, with its stainless steel and lino and washed-out prints of hazy seascapes, vibrated with the news that Malcolm now had a son. It all happened so fast and has never stopped.

Last Saturday, they took Martin to the Planetarium at Mawson Lakes. Theresa bought half a white chocolate mud cake from the Cheesecake Shop – Martin's favourite – and kept it by her feet in its green and red cardboard box. Then they ate all of it on the lawn afterwards, just the three of them; his son didn't have any friends he wanted to bring along. He announced that he would be an astronomer when he grew up, or a space engineer. Malcolm smiled at his son and then he saw that Theresa was looking at him intently, her head lowering slowly – did she want him to say something? Last Saturday felt like months ago now.

Theresa had ordered half a dozen books from Amazon so that they could educate themselves. A label is useful, she'd said, if it helps make you a better parent. God, Malcolm, she'd said, when he confessed he still hadn't read any of 'his half', the ones she'd put on his bedside table with a pad of sticky notes and a pen on top. She had hissed it: *Don't you want to be a better father?* And she clenched her fist and whacked her own forehead.

Shouldn't they at least trust the psychologist, that she would tell them the best thing to do? But he doesn't know why he said this. He doesn't trust Shona. She's been seeing Martin more since the dog disappeared and the nightmares started. It feels like clutching at straws to him. The books are still sitting there now. Malcolm sees them every night, in the moment between his head touching the pillow and the light going out. He can intone them like a prayer: *Pretending to be Normal: Living with Asperger's Syndrome; The Asperger Parent: How to Raise a Child with Asperger Syndrome and*

Maintain your Sense of Humour; and *Can I Tell You about Asperger Syndrome?: A Guide for Friends and Family.*

4. You are not that important

When Malcolm emerges from the cinema into the fading day, there is one new message on his phone. It is from Theresa: *Can u pick up milk pls.* By the time he gets to the car, there is another one, also from Theresa: *M needs excursion $. Get 20 out. Tnks.*

Unbidden memory: the first time he and Theresa made love. Years ago now. The very first time. Front bedroom of the share house. Her flesh, her softness, her smell; thighs, breasts, stomach and something specific; holding her hips in his hands he felt her pelvic bones with his thumbs and he pressed those bones and thought; you could only touch her here, like this, if you were making love to her.

He'll probably lose his hair. People will say – vague and singsong – 'you're looking well', but he already knows, before they've even said it, that he won't be. He'll suffer. It will be ugly, it always is. He's seen too many people to list who died of cancer. Bowel would have to be the worst. And then, when it's all over and you're gone and people have regained their balance after being hit over the head with the idea of mortality, out they will come, one by one, parading their platitudes – 'it was his path,' someone will say, 'he's gone somewhere better,' and the worst: 'it was meant to be.'

Malcolm pinches his nose between his thumb and knuckle, feels the movement of cartilage and the wiry black hairs he's been meaning to pluck. There's a hanky in his pocket, and he pulls it out and briefly rummages around his nostrils. Oh, the tedium ahead; the inevitability of it all. But then it rushes toward him like a huge wave, and for a moment he scrabbles for air. He pushes both hands hard against the dashboard of the car, flexing every muscle through his arms, takes slow, long breaths, steadies himself. He starts the ignition, works through the gears and eases the Subaru out of the carpark. Late afternoon has turned quickly to early evening, and the light has morphed through white and amber and pale grey.

5. Your life is not about you
The engine idles as he waits briefly at traffic lights. He crosses over Adelaide Road and makes a sharp right into the Caltex service station. As he gets out of the car, Malcolm wipes defensively at his cheek with the back of his hand, assuming a bird has excreted on him. But there are no birds in the Caltex. The air is moist with the promise of fog, and there is the lightest rain, barely nameable, easily misread. How quickly it could turn cold up here in the late afternoon. He inhales, and his nostrils fill with earth and diesel and tar and something vague and unpleasant, like an old banana left in a schoolbag.

Inside the service station, a draft of cool air follows him through the electronic glass sliding doors, carrying the mix of outside smells and combining them with the chemicals of lolly snakes and cigarettes. He looks down and notices that the floor is filthy.

As he clenches his fists and feels the cold tips of his fingers against the palms of his hands, he wonders why he had been so keen to get away from the bright sun of the afternoon. Because this is worse; this is morose. Morose, he thinks again and he swallows it, so that the word expands inside him and fills him up. The phrases, 'this is it/this is all there is' appear suddenly in his mind – followed, unadorned, by the word 'nothing'. Malcolm casts them off, strides toward the wall of fridges. He only needs milk and twenty dollars from the ATM, and then he will go home. It's Wednesday, which is tuna pasta. The knowledge of this is comforting – some things stay the same. You can rely on them. But then he wonders, sentimentally, when he is gone will his wife and son still eat tuna pasta on Wednesdays? His scalp prickles and a chill spreads behind his neck and across his shoulders.

He nods at the round-shouldered teenage boy standing behind the green laminex counter, a Jeans for Genes donation box partially obstructing the lad's acne-angry face. The boy nods back, leans across the counter toward the stack of Mars Bars. Malcolm opens the glass door on the left-hand side of the Coca-Cola fridge and reaches in for a two-litre bottle of PURA fat-reduced milk. His fingers wrap around the plastic handle and lift the bottle from the powder-coated shelf.

There is a crashing sound. It is startling and ear-splitting and comes from nowhere. The sound carries no immediate reference to Malcolm's everyday life, or to that of the boy, but it is shocking enough to release instant adrenaline into the bloodstreams of them both. In perfect unison, Malcolm and the boy turn their heads to the glass sliding door that Malcolm entered only seconds before. Both also drop objects: Malcolm the milk; the boy a single Mars Bar. On the security video played back later, police will marvel that the precision of this moment almost looks choreographed. And when played in slow motion, it will look as though a fountain of white milk is erupting from the floor as the plastic bottle splits on impact.

Turning, Malcolm and the boy see a shower of shattering glass hit the ground and skate across the lino. There are quick flashes of dark denim, tightly knit orange hair, large heavy sneakers, something red, the word 'cash', but it sounds more like the bark of an animal than the voice of a human. It will be months before Malcolm realises he still doesn't know what caused the glass to shatter. Neither of them see a gun, although later, piecing together disjointed memory fragments, Malcolm will believe that he did see the gun, will even describe it.

The second explosion is louder, closer. The boy yells out in a high-pitched voice, lunges forward, steps backward and then crumples to the floor behind the counter, as though he is magicked from the scene. Malcolm jolts forward, sees movement and light through the intact windows behind the Jeans for Genes box, and then his feet slip across the milk and give way altogether. When he hits the ground, he feels his chest beating against the wet lino. He feels this, but his face seems strangely absent, and he is aware of a deep ache in his thighs all the way into his hips. His feet are unaccustomedly cold.

The next few seconds are large and blurred, an opus of fast and slow. Malcolm's shoulder is roughly bumped, and his fingers trodden on. Scuttling, shouting, slamming of metal, someone is breathing hard and fast, exhaling in short, even intervals. Then there is silence, as if Malcolm and the milk and the shattered glass and the racks of Starburst and chips and chewies and magazines and DVDs are enclosed together in a bubble, still and clear.

Malcolm crawls commando style toward the counter where the boy lies on the ground grasping at his shoulder, a pool of bright blood growing around his neck and under his arm. He kneels over the boy, looks into his eyes. He understands fully now that the boy is hurt and that he is not. Of everything else that has just happened, Malcolm understands nothing.

'I've been shot! I'm shot! Am I shot?'

The boy's voice has reverted to the early days of first breaking, muffled and awkward, interspersed with tiny squeals. Malcolm sees flashes of bone and gristle through the cone shape that has been blasted into the boy's upper arm, messy and wet now with bright pulsing blood. His yellow and green t-shirt is covered in it, his embroidered nametag unreadable. Without thought, Malcolm tugs the hem of his business shirt from his pants and with both hands rips it apart, popping small buttons into his lap. He pulls the shirt from his body and begins to wrap and stuff the fabric against the boy's open flesh: basic, intuitive first aid.

Then a brash, trilling alarm. Or has this been going the whole time? Malcolm doesn't know, but there are other people now, shouting, and others are treading over glass and rushing toward the counter to where the boy lies still and Malcolm kneels shirtless. Malcolm bends down close to the boy's paling face and rests a palm against his forehead. The boy has deep brown eyes and long eyelashes, the kind his mother's friends probably gushed over when he was small. His open eyes hold the skerrick of a question, but mostly they are calm and resigned.

Malcolm bends closer and whispers something into the boy's ear, but it is drowned out by the growing commotion and the sirens.

He strokes the boy's hair like a father might. He tightens his grip around the boy's arm, his own hand wet and red and white-knuckled and, he thinks absently, who will make sense of all this? What articles will be read? What clichés will be said? Are there words, he wonders, that can clot blood and seal this wound and stitch the inevitable scar?

He hears a woman's voice gasp above him. She starts to shriek, 'Oh my God! Oh my God!' over and over, and Malcolm wants her to stop. And then a male voice cuts over her, 'Please move out of the way, please move out of the way.'

Goosebumps erupt across Malcolm's chest and down his stomach and arms, and he begins to tremble slightly. But inside, he feels warm. The thumping in his chest has slowed and his heart is beating now at a steady pace: *tock-tock-tock-tock*. Subtle interactions of cellular chemicals are at work – a silent interplay of genes and proteins – seeking to regulate Malcolm's inner world. Re-establish some kind of order.

'You'll be okay,' he whispers and then a little louder, 'you're going to be fine,' and he feels sure, although he cannot be certain, that this time the boy hears it.

DANCING ON YOUR BONES

The morning wasn't supposed to go like this. You had planned it so carefully. Amelia's first session of full-time kindergarten. You'd been looking forward to it, this first stretch of three hours. Oh, how you had wanted this. But now here you are, sitting in your car, unable to leave the kindergarten carpark. Even though you are meant to be somewhere else. Paul was expecting you at nine. This was what you wanted: to have somewhere you were *meant* to be. (You dreamt about Paul again – in those last semi-aroused moments of sleep, before you were consciously accountable for the storyline. But now a vague guilt, like the misery of a tepid bath.)

You left Amelia red-faced and crisscrossed in snot. Her arms were flexed hard, her fingers stretched wide and pleading, her tiny body wrangling against the arms of no-nonsense, blonde-ponytailed Marni. You tried to get close, to comfort your daughter, but in the throng of limbs and Amelia's crying, it seemed impossible, so you just stood there.

'Leave,' Marni had instructed, not looking at you properly. 'Just leave.' As though you were the alcoholic at a family barbecue.

You drop your forehead against the Holden lion in the steering wheel's centre, and your lashes bend against the hard black plastic. What choice did you have, with everyone watching like that, but to leave? Your shoulders had trembled as you fiddled clumsily with the newfangled safety lock on the gate. Now, you wonder if you should go back in and take Amelia out. You'll have to ring Paul and tell him you won't be coming in. You chew on your lip.

All the other mums seemed to know one another already. You overheard 'girls' night in' and 'pink champagne', and you saw one of them lean in and brush away a little something on another's cheekbone.

No one could break into that.

You pull down the sun visor and slide open the mirror: your throat is a map of flushing pink from collarbone to collarbone. It was just frustrating. You hit the steering wheel with your palm. Frustrating. All that gooey neon claggy stuff in plastic tubs, those buckets of stubby chalk, the blobs of paint that made you think of coloured meringue, the construction blocks, and the wire racks filled with every sized recyclable container and carton ready to be cut and glued and taped and ... surely – you thought – surely Amelia was going to feel like Goldilocks encountering the artefacts of baby bear; one of those 'Finally: this is where I belong' feelings. You've spent thirty-eight years longing for that feeling, imagining it on your skin, naively hoping to taste it in your mouth like a new-flavoured Life Saver. But no: Amelia had hung back. Her small white chin resting on her collarbone, her clear blue eyes straining upwards, her tight little fingers grasping for a fistful of your skirt. You noticed the *We are one, We are many* poster on the kindy wall, and all the brightly coloured Reconciliation posters.

Your husband had suggested you offer to help with Art activities, maybe on the days you weren't volunteering at The Shed. You could offer to do dot paintings with them, he said. A little talk about Aboriginal art. They'd jump at it, he said. Kindies love a bit of PC stuff.

But with Amelia carrying on like that, you hadn't managed a single conversation with anyone.

You flick up the sun visor and pull on your seatbelt, click it in.

A bevy of mums has congregated around a black Prado, laughing and chatting and jangling car keys, toddlers perched on their jutted hips; second children, maybe thirds. They throw their heads back and show their teeth, and you imagine them saying '*I know!*' over and over.

'This is a great opportunity for you to meet people, Don.' Roger's words this morning. You watched as your husband buttered toast, his tie tucked behind his shoulder. He'd already been for a run around the wetlands. (You hate 'Don' more than you hate 'Donna.')

You think of Roger's advice as 'Rogerisms', and lately you've shortened that to 'Risms'. You store them in your mind with his pet turns of phrase and favourite words in a little corner marked *Risms*. Lately, it's been '... around the issue of ...' It's consultant speak, but to you, it's a Rism.

You know that your husband only wants to help.

An image flashes into your mind. Roger is wearing army fatigues. He's barricaded himself in the Council chambers behind a wall of orange plastic blocks, the kind they use in all the roadworks. In loincloths and carrying spears, hordes of angry Aboriginal men are poised to attack him. The image amuses you. It is ridiculous. But then you wonder: is it racist? Sometimes, it's hard to know.

Roger's consultancy with Mount Barker Council was the reason you moved here – a long-term proposition, with talks of a twenty-year plan. They needed someone, urgently, to help them manage all the stakeholders, to focus on the infrastructure, which, by their own admission, was a dog's breakfast. Clearly there weren't enough roundabouts or traffic lights or carparks in the central business district of town. The roads were from another era: potholed, narrow, constantly gridlocked. Land around the town was being sliced up and dug into fake lakes and ill-conceived wetlands, hastily built houses plonked in between. The whole area was looking like the sandpit of a boisterous child. Everything was bursting at the seams with the population growth, even the hospital.

'The *change* had to change,' was the way Roger put it, which the Council apparently liked. They said it showed a man who at least wasn't 'anti-change'. He said it sounded like they needed someone to '*manage* the change', and they liked that too.

What they really needed was someone who could at least have a conversation about environmental sustainability, someone with the balls to get the best possible outcomes from the state government, the wherewithal to manage developers. No one mentioned native title back then. Everyone had forgotten about that. Now Roger was saying things like, 'We need to have a conversation around the issue of Aboriginal heritage', because a native title claim had been lodged. A little red herring, Roger said, and it paid to remember that anyone could make an application to the Supreme Court if they wanted. It had nothing to do with Council anyway, he said. It was federal. But developers got nervy; it was only natural.

Put it this way, Roger explained: expect extra bottles of Grange Hermitage. And he winked across the coffee table. Behind his head, on the buffet, already stood three bottles, like pieces in an unspoken board game.

Last night you were grating potatoes for Amelia's fritters, and Roger stood behind you, rubbing his thumb down the side of your waist. Small rolls of fat caught between the fabric of your shirt and your skin, and you wriggled free.

'You'd know something about this, wouldn't you, Don?' Roger cocked his head. He was looking at you differently, as though trying to imagine your younger self. 'I always thought the Peramangk people died from smallpox in 1836,' he said.

It was true. You had studied Aboriginal Art, years ago, and you did know one or two things about the importance of land, spirituality and what have you. You'd never heard the word 'Peramangk' spoken aloud, but now that you had, it did ring a bell.

'Maybe our flash new sign gave someone ideas,' Roger said, and he smirked into his red wine.

No, you'd seen 'Peramangk' recently, not just on the new

sign at the wetlands. You explained to Roger that there were lots of different Aboriginal groups, lots of different languages, maybe more than three hundred. Plus all the dialects. You'd learnt a few Pitjantjatjara words once. You couldn't recall any, but then you remembered *Uwa* for 'yes'. Your lips made a point with the 'w' as the memory surfaced.

You didn't know much about native title. The Aboriginal students used to make a joke – it was right after Mabo then. 'You got a pool?' they'd ask. 'Nah? Well, we don't want ya fucken backyard then.' Rollicking laughter.

You had considered telling that joke to Roger last night.

~

One of the mums chatting around the Prado glances over, and you watch as the toddler on her hip pulls at her hair. You close your eyes and say 'Peramangk' out loud. Then you say 'Donna' and then 'Amelia'. You and Roger agreed on Amelia. You were pleased; you felt it was the opposite sort of name to yours. Your own name is like a deadbeat apology, a dong on the head. Donna. Dong. 'Amelia,' you say again. Hearing your own voice in the car sounds odd, as though it belongs to something inanimate: the car seat, or the dashboard, something made of plastic, not blood and bone. You wonder what crying would sound like. You don't remember the last time you cried. You get the rash a lot. And the weight on your chest that makes it hard to breathe.

Amelia looked so skinny and pale next to all those other children in the kindergarten. She's not like you. You're an apple: rounded tummy, larger than average breasts, not much of a bottom. Okay legs. You've seen men look at them, but mostly they look at your breasts. You believe you've seen Paul look at them – surreptitiously – when you pop into his office to say you've arrived or to see if he needs anything posted. You wish you were a pear. Or a banana, like Roger's mother, who intonates the words 'slim' and 'trim' as though they are virtues. On and on she goes about Lite n' Easy and how it works for her, as if she's being paid to do live ads for them. And yoga. Tina swears by yoga. Every time you see her you lay bets with yourself, because this you can count on: no matter what, she will find a way to show you her downward dog.

You turn the key in the ignition, and the sound of the engine causes all the mums at the Prado to turn toward your car and then dart their eyes around to locate their small children. The woman with the toddler seems to be looking directly at you and she smiles and you smile back, but then you realise that she is mid-conversation with one of the other mums, that she isn't smiling at you at all.

You drive out of the carpark and onto the road, where large gum trees lean over and threaten to drop their limbs. Blasted Sig trees, Roger calls them. The Council deems them 'significant', which means they can't be cut down without a permit. It always makes you nervous when Amelia plays under them in the reserve. The leaves pass mottled shadows across the bonnet of your car so that the duco sparkles with sunlight and then darkens: light then dark, light then dark, light then dark. You tighten your grip around the steering wheel and concentrate on the road ahead. There is a saying that you have tried to forget, but it comes back to you, often. You hear it in your mind as vividly as if it is spoken aloud, and the voice is mocking.

They say that white people living or working in Aboriginal communities are one of three things: mercenary, missionary or misfit.

No one would ever suggest you were a mercenary. Your fear of being one of the others was partly why you didn't want that job as art liaison officer at Ernabella.

You slow down to twenty-five on Gawler Street where they're putting in a temporary roundabout. This is the reason you enjoy your work at The Shed, even though you are only a volunteer. Because around Paul, and Markayla too, you don't feel as though you are one of those three things. And even though your desk in the front foyer is collected from hard rubbish and peeling at the edges, you feel good sitting there. You feel as though you are part of something. The Shed is the public interface of the Community Centre, run by the Council. You like to forget it was Roger's idea that you volunteer there in the first place.

'You've got some perfectly decent admin skills, Donna. There'd be no harm in honing them up, in a volunteer capacity at least.' He kissed the top of your head. 'All good employment begins with the spirit of the volunteer. I firmly believe that.'

You'd always suspected that Roger was anti-unionist.

You feel so alive when you are at The Shed. You would like to think, and you will probably even explain it so to Paul when you arrive (not probably; you will), that Amelia is like Roger: tentative, lacking a little in charisma and social confidence. It will be easy to say she is like Roger and to lightly laugh about it, to couch it in an air of affection, like ruffling up the hair on a dog. Even though it isn't true, and you know it. Amelia might have Roger's physicality: 'Look at her thighs! Just like Roger!' Tina says, as if you've won the jackpot with that. But Amelia is not like Roger. The unappealing quality in your child, the social inadequacy that makes you flinch, that repels and tenderises you with equal ferocity – this quality is not inherited from your husband. Amelia is like you.

And yet, if you'd taken that art liaison job – it seems unbelievable now that you were even offered it – how different your life would be. It is almost impossible to imagine, but sometimes you try. Romanticising it, naturally. You would have had a *job* for starters, maybe even a career. You'd be interesting and confident; the kind of woman who is comfortable with her own body, the kind of woman who has a 'style'. You'd be political and articulate and have a skin name, probably – given to you by the community – and friends and family would say that you were *amaaazing*, and you'd protest that you were not, and then you'd draw back on some kind of herbal cigarette. You definitely wouldn't have been one of those 'fly in/fly out' bureaucrat-style white fellas who pay next-to-nothing for the dot paintings and then sell them on to a gallery at The Rocks for five hundred times more. You heard a lot about those. Once, on a sunny afternoon, all the mercenaries and missionaries and misfits were sitting outside the Aboriginal Studies building on the outskirts of uni, and you said, 'Those art dealers are racist pricks, total pricks.' The others chimed, 'I reckon', 'yeah' and 'yeah', like a chorus.

No, you would have been ethical. And a highly respected elder in the community called Daisy would say: 'We only want white fellas here like you, Donna May.' And you would be all diplomatic and only mildly patronising when you'd say: 'C'mon, Daisy, there are plenty of good white fellas around the place. You just haven't met many.' And then you'd all fall about laughing.

You lifted that word for word from an overheard conversation – you weren't the white woman. It was Cheryl Hammond. Cheryl needed someone to take over her job at Ernabella while she stayed in Adelaide to look after her sick mother. They were desperate for a replacement, desperate enough to offer the job to all the Diploma grads, all seven of you.

What was Cheryl, you wonder? Mercenary, missionary or misfit? Or was she truly just Cheryl?

You had wanted to be an artist. But the faculty didn't like your portfolio. They sat side by side on a long, narrow table, and the woman in the dead centre with spiky hair and a Canadian accent wanted to know, 'What is the political framework here?' You looked over the canvases you'd laid out before them, all your still-lifes in oils, and you remember your bottom lip felt strangely thick. They said your work lacked *theoretical context*, which you understood at the time to mean it wasn't feminist enough. It was the early 90s, and everyone was doing stuff with photography. Invariably it was an image of a naked woman gagged in some way, her mouth plastered with gaffer tape or something more heinous. It was close-ups of road kill and dismembered plastic dolls. Macabre and disturbing things to make people *think*.

You wanted beautiful. All you wanted were the skills to create something beautiful, like all those great artists you loved: Michelangelo, Monet, Matisse, Manet and, of course, the M exception: Chagall. The first time you saw a Chagall – it was *The Lovers* – you ached for it.

Your rejection from the visual arts faculty was around the time of the exhibition. You'd been invited to contribute something, along with a handful of others, after the WEA course you'd done to get a body of work together for the portfolio.

Your idea had come in the middle of the night. You still remember. It had struck you as brilliant: a rush in your throat, pins pricking across your forearms. As your eyes adjusted to the cool dark of your small, bare-bricked room, you scribbled furiously into your bedside journal, kept there for such a moment.

Realised, it felt immediately barren – the two easels side by side looked inconsequential in the large space, and the slab of empty butcher's paper bulldog-clipped to one didn't create the accessible, informal energy you'd imagined. It felt amateurish and unsophisticated. In the middle of the two easels you'd placed a round table and, on that, an interesting collection of fruit and vegetables, piled artfully across a silver tray and spilling from a ceramic bowl. Next to the bowl, a wooden box was filled with brand-new paints and brushes, pastels and pristine sticks of charcoal. The first easel held a canvas of your own most recent work. A still life in oils: apples and persimmons in a blue and white Chinese bowl, a small nest holding three speckled eggs of a quail. You were pleased with it. But it was more than a simple still life. You were trying to say something, too. You were trying to say that Art was for everyone, that it wasn't exclusive and shouldn't be roped off. You were trying to say that people shouldn't be made to feel inadequate in the face of it (for, in fact, this is how you felt). You claimed to rile at the preciousness of it all, and the *Mona Lisa* was your primary example. When you spoke about it, your heart rate went up, and you'd get the rash, especially when you made reference to 'the masses' or when you said 'capital A, Art'. The idea for your exhibition came first, the philosophy behind it came second, and you wondered later if that was the fundamental flaw.

On that early morning alone in your bed in that little unit you were renting, you had imagined small crowds forming as people took gracious turns experimenting with their creativity, inspired by the tools and example you'd provided. You imagined whisking each finished sheet of butcher's paper off the easel and displaying them on the wall behind, to further inspire others to have a go.

You invited people to help themselves to the supplies in the wooden box. *Don't be Afraid to Make your Mark!* your poster read underneath the blank butcher's paper, followed by, *DO touch the Art.*

DO suck my Cock someone had scrawled in purple pastel #15, with a crude depiction of a penis underneath. Under the comment, *Fuck me with a cucumber*, someone called Carly had signed her name. On the blank easel you'd provided, people had strewn only words: crude words. A good number just signed their name; there was a lot of so and so *woz here.*

As it turned out, you fundamentally believed that Art should be roped off.

~

The Diploma in Aboriginal Art was all that was left when you didn't get into the Bachelor of Visual Arts. You didn't need a portfolio for the Diploma, an interview, a TER, or anything at all. You were a mature age student. You'd been working in a mobile sandwich van. You had to do something.

They were desperate for enrolments in Aboriginal Studies; enrolments meant funding. You were desperate to be enrolled in anything. You knew nothing about Aboriginal people, even less about Torres Strait Islanders. You asked the girl sitting next to you on the first day if she was a half-caste.

'I'm Aboriginal,' she said, 'No one's a half-caste.'

This memory was as fresh and recoverable as snap-frozen peas.

Some things you never forget. Things that people say. They pop up in your head at unlikely and unexpected moments, years later, as if your subconscious is holding them down underwater like a big cluster of buoys and then – *pop!* – one is released to the surface where it sits for a while, innocent and unassuming in the glaring midday sun.

Like this, overheard from your change room in a Jeans West store in 1998:

'My girlfriend asked me how she'd know if she'd had an orgasm ... can you believe that?! God, I told her: You'll *know*.'

This pops to the surface often, especially the last bit, 'You'll *know.'* Because you don't know. You've never known. And you want to know. You've been feeling lately as though you are running out of time with this.

~

'Isn't it funny,' you say to Paul when you put your head around his door to let him know you've arrived, 'isn't it funny how no matter how well you've prepared your child for their first day at kindergarten, it still ends in tears?' You flatten your mouth and feign a sad face.

Paul is sitting in his black vinyl executive chair behind the kidney-shaped director's desk. He raises his hands from the keyboard and pulls them toward his Santa stomach, linking his fingers across the midpoint.

Paul doesn't have children but he's a social worker and you know he's interested in this stuff. You've found him so easy to talk to, and you've only been here five weeks. Two afternoons a week: Tuesdays when you take Amelia to the Community Centre's Come 'n' Try occasional care, and Thursdays when Roger comes home early, especially. You find Paul easier to talk to than anyone. Ever. It is startling and calming: strangely both. You marvel at your ability to link ideas and sentences together when you're with him. You even think, when you're with him, that sometimes you might be funny. You feel braver all the time.

'Oh?' He tilts his head and looks for your eyes, pries them gently into his own. You look straight at him and then down at your hands and back up.

'Are you okay? About being here? I hope you didn't feel as

though you had to come, just because you said you would. We really appreciate it, Donna, but I hope you didn't leave your daughter there if it didn't feel right for you?'

You love that: 'if it didn't feel right for you'.

'No, no, it's fine, really.' He watches you closely, tilts his head as if he's unconvinced and waiting for more. You love this also.

'Okay – I admit I sat in the carpark for a while getting myself together afterwards ...' You smile. 'But I was pretty sure she'd be fine once I left, you know. Sometimes you just have to leave, so long as they're safe, obviously, so that they can find their own inner resources.' You don't even know where you got that. You wonder if you just made that up. You add: 'It builds resilience, I think. She's quite sensitive and she struggles a bit socially – like her father, I suppose – but she was in good hands this morning. Hey, did you want a cup of tea? I think I'm going to have one.'

He makes a funny gurgling sound in his throat. 'You don't have to make me tea, sheesh! I'll get *you* one, it's the least I can do. Can't promise Earl Grey or anything, but I'm sure there's a Lipton's out there.'

'Oh, there's plenty of Lipton's,' you tell Paul. 'I restocked them last Thursday with petty cash. And I hope that's okay. You were at that regional manager's meeting thingee.'

'That was you? God, we need someone here with some initiative. Thanks for that, Donna. You've no idea, I really mean that.' He pushes himself away from the desk, stands. 'Yep, I think you're right, Donna, time for a smoko.'

Paul doesn't smoke, which is good. Smoko is just another of his idiosyncratic, down-to-earth phrases. Americans are 'septic tanks', his sister his 'skin blister', and when you had the sausage sizzle on the last day of 'Emotional Boundaries for Women,' he asked you to pass him the 'dead horse'. Carefree. When you are around Paul, you feel it too. When you are with Paul, you can't help asking yourself: why don't I feel this way with Roger? With Roger you feel as though both of you are waiting for you to grow up, to become your true self. Ironically, this was the reason you married Roger.

You back out of the doorway to Paul's office, and he turns his palms up as he manoeuvres past you in the narrow hallway. A tingle at the base of your spine as you follow him into the kitchenette, your eyes fixed on the thin plait snaking down his back.

Paul is one of those men whose clothes are like a trademark. Every day you've been here it is the same: dark denim jeans held below that stomach with a thick brown leather belt, a large Harley-Davidson emblem at the front, black polyester shirt pulled tight and tucked in, twenty-odd-year-old elasticised R.M. Williams boots. His thinning uncut hair pulled always into this low plait, fastened every time with thin red elastic. You imagine a little clay pot filled with red elastics on his bathroom vanity in Croydon – Paul commutes up the freeway to work, while most of the traffic is going down. You imagine his fingers ducking in and out of the mousy strands, precise and familiar, every morning. You wonder if he wears the plait to bed.

Nothing – *nothing* – about Paul is attractive to you. He is the opposite in every way to your husband, and the opposite of what you have always *thought* of as an attractive man.

Roger is trim, contained, groomed and shaven, simply and fashionably dressed: a suit during the week, smart casual on the weekend. 'Smart casual' is practically a Rism. Your husband smells of freshly ironed cotton and Aramis Classic. Paul smells of strong coffee, a tinge of body odour mixed with some sort of sweet aftershave, spices you're unsure of, maybe – whatever people put in curries. An earthy mix, slightly rancid.

And yet here you are: wildly, shamefully, strangely attracted to Paul.

You've been making up all sorts of fantasies about him. In them, you use words and phrases that you've seen in public toilet cubicles, ones that were scrawled over your artwork all those years ago. Sometimes you shock yourself. Sometimes you wake in the night so aroused by your dreams of Paul, you discover yourself thrashing and thrusting against the mattress. When you realise where you are and what is happening, you lie perfectly still, horrified and electric, while your breathing continues fast and shallow. Roger lies next to you, sleeping peacefully.

You don't understand it but neither can you deny it. And now that Amelia has officially started 'full time', you'll be able to volunteer at The Shed more – most days, in fact. The thought brings an immediate sense of lightness and warmth, but then you remember the drama of the morning at the kindergarten and you feel as though a small animal has clambered up your chest and is clawing at your throat. You were worried when Roger took the consultancy. You were worried that moving up here wasn't going to be a good thing for Amelia. You were worried that she'd struggle to make new friends.

Roger did the research. He said that Gladeview Park

estate, on the outskirts of town, was the most desirable. Blocks couldn't be further divided, which was important, because you didn't want to live in a perpetual building site. You bought an established house in Cherrybrook Close with wide verandahs, 9-foot ceilings, a Jag kitchen and central air. Perfectly symmetrical cumquat trees in matching pots on either side of the front door. 'Views to die for,' Roger said as he showed you the pictures on realestate.com. 'We'll get a dog,' he said as he flicked to the wide-angled photo of the backyard, and then: 'Children shouldn't be in cities. They should be in nature.' (Almost a Rism.) At each of the three barbecues you'd hosted in the initial flurry to network, Roger mystifyingly asked the guests: 'I mean, who wants their kid to find a syringe in the local playground?'

Amelia had never found a syringe in any playground.

The Sophie Barlow story was in all the papers when you first moved up here – the local teenage girl who was lured by a paedophile on Facebook. The details so disturbing that some mornings it made you ill to read about it. The caffeine from your breakfast coffee churned your stomach up like a rip in the ocean, tugging you out somewhere unknown and frightening. The bewildered look on that father's face on the TV news, and the mother, who couldn't even look up at the camera, as though she was the one on trial. You tell yourself that they mustn't have been watching closely enough, that it must be their fault. You'll never let Amelia do Facebook, or anything like it, you said to Roger.

'She's *four*,' Roger kept saying, as though you were too.

And now here you are sipping on your Lipton tea, all

the paedophile stories in the paper dried up and practically forgotten, and you're keying in The Shed's Term 3 course guide.

Thursdays 9.30am – 11.30am 2 weeks commencing 1 September. Have you ever wondered what Facebook is all about? Markayla will help you discover the joys of becoming a Facebooker.

You scan the list. You wouldn't mind enrolling in some of these courses yourself – 'Publisher', 'Navigate the World Wide Web like a Pro', 'PowerPoint', 'Excel', 'Make Chinese Spring Rolls', 'Don't Be Afraid of Pastry!'

You are terrified of pastry. What you do know is this: you want to be on the delivery side of these small and sad courses, even though you lack the skills of almost every one. When all of the town's fringe dwellers and forgotten people – the pensioners, the mentally ill and the homeless – wander in and pick up pamphlets for Centrelink and the library and the local nature walks and the Laratinga Wetlands, you use an overly enthusiastic voice about the fun they could have enrolling in one of The Shed's courses. And not only are they super cheap, you tell them, they are even *free* on a health-care card. You actually say 'super cheap'.

~

Roger turns out to be right about the spirit of the volunteer.

Before you leave to pick Amelia up, Paul and Markayla come into the foyer and stand by your desk looking pleased.

You glance up from your tatty reception desk, and Paul leans across and lightly touches your forearm, instigating a shiver that travels to your shoulder and into the back of your neck. He says, 'Donna, we really appreciate all the work you do here. Everything you've done. To be completely honest, I didn't even realise how many little admin jobs weren't getting done until you came and took the initiative and actually did them.' Markayla rolls her eyes and starts nodding her head in a little rhythm. She wears skinny jeans with a soft shirt. The tiny silver dot in her nose bobs up and down.

'Look,' says Paul, 'we've decided to apply for a grant to employ you for, say, two mornings a week. It's not much, I know. I can't promise anything, and it'd probably only be casual in the first instance, but ... if you're interested?' He raises his eyebrows and pulls his lips into a tight smile, and then puffs his cheeks out like a fish. A little unbecoming, but a little endearing too.

'Yes,' you say. 'Great.' Yes, you're interested. More than interested. You smile and breathe out through your nose.

Markayla gives one last nod and says, 'Good job,' and then walks back down the hallway, leaving you alone with Paul.

He watches Markayla go, turns back and says, 'Great.' Then he leans over and sort of pushes your shoulder, which makes you wobble a bit, and you both laugh. He is still smiling as he turns for his own office, but then he takes a step back toward you, leaving one foot raised slightly off the floor. Comical, seeing such a beefy man in that pose, as though he's attempting a ballet manoeuvre, and you laugh again, but it's only you laughing now.

'Hey, Donna, um, you know that I'm ... I'm a *bear*, right?'
He is still smiling, but it's quizzical as well, and he's shrugging.
The foot still hovering midair.

You feel yourself redden as your mind searches frantically
for this reference. Bear, a bear, a big grizzly bear. We're going
on a bear hunt, we're gonna catch a big one. We're not scared!

'Um, ah, okay, yeah.' You giggle. You feel the rash creep
down your neck and across your throat.

Paul clicks the fingers of each hand in quick succession and
then slaps one palm onto the balled fist of the other: *click, click,
bam*. 'Cool,' he says. Finally, his foot drops to the ground and
he ducks back into his office, hitting his open palms against the
doorframe as he goes like some kind of one-man band.

Bear: you type it straight into the search engine. After *bears
are mammals of the family Ursidae*, there are the Chicago Bears
and then the LGBT slang term for members of the homosexual
subculture bears. You type in LGBT: lesbian, gay, bisexual and
transgender. God. Right. Okay, right. You flick back to the first
Wikipedia entry. A line of heat flares down the middle of your
scalp as though someone has set your hair on fire. You feel it
radiate along your back and into your thighs, calves, ankles.
Moisture pools behind your ears and under your arms, rolling
down the underside of your favourite hibiscus print shirt.

You thought gay men wore tight black jeans and little
designer cardigans and talked about fashion. Was the plait a
clue?

Paul is gay: subculture special hairy slang gay. Okay, that's
okay: and you don't know whether you said that aloud or
thought it. You're not sure, but it's perfectly okay.

~

When you arrive back at the kindergarten, Amelia is sitting on the carpet with all the other children, a pile of paintings by her side, gum-leaf prints by the looks of it. Her expression is a mixture of pride and bewilderment, as if she's just killed something for her dinner. And she appears to have made some friends, two fat girls called Sophia and Francesca: identical twins.

Maybe Amelia *isn't* like you.

All the way home, she sings 'dem bones dem bones dem dry bones' from her booster on the back seat. As the roller door rumbles down behind you in the garage, you see that she is fast asleep, a line of drool running down her soft chin.

~

You arrive at The Shed the next morning and unlock the front door with the new key Paul has cut for you. It looks like he's come and gone – all the lights are on and your computer is on too. You put your bag on the desk and sit down in the chair. You breathe in and out slowly, roll your head around a few times, clench and release your fingers, as though you're trying on new skin.

Amelia had spotted the twins in the kindergarten carpark this morning. You and the mum introduced yourselves in front of the *Children Don't Bounce!* sign. Susan Hillman. She does admin for the accountant in the main street. You work at the Council, you told her.

The Shed feels different this morning. Knowing that soon you might be paid to be here, it all feels different: more appealing, more significant. But you also notice the shabbiness, really see it: the melamine strip peeling from your desk, the ugly water stain on the ceiling above you, the scuffed carpet and spots where the nylon threads have come loose and are bunched together like spaghetti. You wonder if they might also apply for funds to buy one of those nice new desks from Harvey Norman, a dark grey one with a return, perhaps. You notice that there is a handwritten note on your keyboard:

Donna, I'm at strengths-based l'ship training all day 2day. Markayla will come in b4 you leave. Have a good one! P
Ps. I put in the request – if you reboot, u should have LAN access.

So, you're alone this morning. You restart the computer and, while the hard drive hums, you pull from your handbag the things you've brought from home.

There's a framed photo of Amelia taken in the front garden of your old house on her fourth birthday. Second: a photo of Roger holding Amelia in the hospital, maybe an hour after she was born. You were still in theatre when it was taken, but you like the expression on his face: utter helplessness. When you look at this photo, you know that Roger will never leave you. Third: your favourite mug. It's white china and has a photograph of the *Mona Lisa* holding a small red card that says 'Keep Calm and Smile'. You're going to leave it here, even when you're not. It will be like a stake in the land, a little flag that says: Donna's desk.

Paul was right. You have email now, and the Council intranet, which means Paul and Markayla won't have to keep printing things out for you. They'll just email. They've copied you in on several already, and you notice that they both have the same signature format, the same italicised paragraph underneath their phone numbers. Yes: this is where you've seen the word 'Peramangk' before. You had a feeling that it was somewhere here, at The Shed. At your *work*, you correct, and reposition your bottom on the chair. You highlight and copy the paragraph, and then click around for a while until you find the spot where you can create your own signature. You type *Donna May*, return, *Administration*, return, *The Shed Community Centre*, return, *Mount Barker Council*, return, *South Australia*, return, and then paste. There it is.

> *I acknowledge that this land is the traditional ancestral land of the Peramangk People. I acknowledge the deep feelings of attachment and relationship of the Peramangk people to this land and their ongoing custodianship.*

You read it back a couple of times. You like it. You like the look of it. You like the 'I acknowledge' part and the words 'deep' and 'relationship' and 'custodianship' and the way they make everything feel safe and dramatic at the same time. And as though you are really part of it all now, like a proper employee with an email signature that means something. You wonder if you should ask Paul about a name badge, so that if someone emails first, they'll be able to put a face to a name when they actually come in and see you here in the foyer.

You adjust the two pictures on your desk so that they turn in slightly toward each other. You pick up the mug and move it from the left side of your keyboard to the right side, and then back again. You angle it a little, so the handle is positioned for easy reach without having to slide from your chair. In a moment, you'll go to the kitchenette and fill the kettle. You'll make yourself a cup of tea.

But first you want to play with the colours of your email set-up. You're thinking green for the text and maybe a border, a scroll in a darker green perhaps, which will run down the side. You didn't realise that there were so many colours on the palette ·to choose from. You can even create your own variations and shades by moving your cursor around on a colour wheel. You're thinking more mauves now, mauves and deep reds.

The telephone rings on your desk. In essence, this is your job: to answer the telephone, to field enquiries. But the ringing is so abrupt, so loud and somehow unexpected, that you gasp, and your hand moves involuntarily to your heart.

~

That evening, Roger is out of sorts. He opens a bottle of wine but doesn't pour it, flicks through his phone, sits, stands and sits again. Amelia is full of beans. You watch her from the kitchen as she races around the living area and up the hallway on her spindly legs, singing 'Dem Bones' and 'Open Shut Them', and yelling at you that she's really called Francesca. 'Francesca,' you repeat, using your calm mother voice, 'that sounds a bit like Amelia.' 'No, it doesn't,' she shrieks, 'it's com-plete-ly diff-er-ent!' You've never known her like this, so full of energy, almost unhinged.

Roger stands at the kitchen bench where you are stacking the dishwasher, and he rubs his hands roughly over his eyes and then back and forth through his closely cropped, silver-tipped hair. He pulls his mouth apart like a lion about to yawn, and makes a guttural sound. You try to imagine Paul sitting at home. You imagine him beating his chest and growling, bear-like. Maybe he's taken out the red elastic and he's forking his fingers through his hair. You feel a little ridiculous, imagining this, and also strangely pleased, but you don't know why. You are a mystery, even to yourself.

You move toward Roger and rub your knuckles into the small of his back and then firmly up his spine with the side of your hand.

He rolls his shoulders around appreciatively. 'Oh yeah. Up a bit. That's it. Yup, that's it. You were always good at that.' Then, 'God,' he says, while you knead into his shoulders, and Amelia ducks around under your legs. 'I swear to God, I'd never even heard of the bloody Peramangk people before we moved up here. Never heard of them, never seen them ...' He laughs, incredulous, which makes Amelia laugh too. 'These people reckon they've got a claim on this whole town, starting at the Summit, which is meant to be a sacred site and then right across the Mt Lofty Ranges. It's nonsense, not even an ambit claim, more of a philosophical point. But I've been getting calls about it all day. Not only from developers either. I've had calls from government, media ... People are talking about an enquiry. It's nonsense.'

You don't know what to say to Roger about this. What he is saying seems vague and unreal, but also strangely appealing. You wonder if there might be cave paintings to show the sacred sites.

'We shouldn't have funded that sign,' Roger says.

You move your hands to the base of your husband's hairline and push your fingers into the knots in his neck. Roger turns around to look at you and then rubs his hands over your shoulders, making the sleeves of your hibiscus shirt ruffle up and then down again. 'You know what they should do? The government should give approval to build a bloody estate on the Summit,' Roger says. 'That'd fix it all up. That's the real Mount Barker, let's be honest. Just move on. Build the nicest development there. Make it special. Call it "Mount Barker Estate". Or call it "Peramangk Estate". You know, Don, that's not so stupid. That could be a win-win.'

You pour yourself a glass of wine from the opened bottle on the bench and take it to the couch. Amelia runs up and jumps on your lap. You raise your glass high over her head and wait for the wine to settle before you set it down on the side table. She straddles your lap and digs her fingers into the fleshy part of your hips. You reshuffle your seat; wonder if you should at least try Lite n' Easy.

'Yaaar hip bones connected to ya, thigh bone,' Amelia sings, 'and ya thigh bone's connected to ya, leg bone.' She runs her own bony fingers up and down your body as though you're a piano. 'Look, Mama,' she says, 'I'm dancing on your bones.'

She tips her head back and laughs maniacally so that you see all her little teeth from their milky undersides. Then she flops back down and splays her chest against yours. You feel her wet mouth on your neck, and you wrap your arms easily around her skinny body.

MAY TWENTIETH

I'm sitting in the blue chair, school laptop on my knees, in my father's private room. Private ones are hard to get – you might have to be dying. I have just finished the Cherry Ripe. It tasted more like the air in here than the thing itself; warm, bland, stale, sad, expectant. There is no easy way to say this, so I will just do it: my father *is* dying. He might even die today – he probably will – which sounds horrible, but it's not as horrible as you'd think. The doctor said that we should say our *goodbyes*, so I said it: *Goodbye, Dad*. The next day I said: *Goodbye, then*. But I'm not going to just keep doing that. I'm wondering if most things aren't as horrible as you'd think, once they happen to you, or at least once you've had time to get used to them. It depends on how you *look* at them, and I'll get to that.

Well, that's the beginning, the first paragraph. You will see the orientation; we are in a hospital room. You know the narrator; me (Martin Wheeler). I haven't told you when – it's Friday 20 May but you probably guessed that from the title.

You asked for an engaging title, Mrs K, and I haven't found this easy. I have six others in reserve. You would have seen five adjectives to describe the air in the room. You can tick those off on the assessment sheet right now, I suppose.

I know you want to see that I understand the conventions of a narrative, and I do, I really do.

The air being expectant; you might have thought that strange. When someone you know is dying – when they will die any *minute* – everywhere you go feels expectant. That 'something big is going to happen' feeling. Not like Christmas, obviously, but like it. Colours look different, brighter, especially blues and greens. That is not an original observation – I read it somewhere or heard it in a song but I've found that it is true. And your skin feels tickly if it gets touched.

Every day for the past week they've said it could be 'today'. That's why I'm here, even though it's a school day, because someone needs to be here and Aunty Pippa has taken Mum for a break. Mum was here all night.

This room has the biggest expectant feeling of all because my father is in it.

But it's not as bad as you'd think.

I call my theory *Eyes 1* and *Eyes 2*, but I suspect I'll come up with something better than that eventually.

~

Take the wall. Stare at the wall above my father's head (don't think about him for the moment). It's just a blank wall, hard and solid, painted a light beige. It's nothing but a wall. You are staring at the wall with *Eyes 1* – it takes a moment to go into it completely but once you do, be very careful because it could swallow you up. Staring at it with *Eyes 1*, the wall is not just a wall, but literally it is *just* a wall: a stupid, useless, dumb wall. There is nothing about it except itself. Nothing, and that's the point. Keep going. Keep staring at it with *Eyes 1*. You'll start to feel desperate; a rat scavenging in the wetlands; a starving person willing to eat mouldy, rotten food. If you've ever been in *Eyes 1* long enough, you'll know what I'm talking about: the sadness, the desperate feeling. You could fall down a dark tunnel in *Eyes 1*, suffocate in quicksand, become tangled in riverweeds.

Okay, now *Eyes 2*. Pull your focus back, now look at the wall and *imagine* that you are looking at it – that is the key. Please don't give up on this. It's not as weird as it sounds. And I know you, of all people, could do it.

Imagining the wall. You need to breathe slowly and think of something to imagine about the wall; it really could be anything. You could think about who built it. (Was it Barry? Tony? Bob?) What exact beige is that from the paint chart? (Biscuit? Vanilla cream? Caramel whisper?) What picture would you hang there? (A sunset? A rainforest? A field of flowers?) *Eyes 2* could take you anywhere. And then you find that you're not just staring at a wall. You're interested in the wall and maybe happy, in a way.

My mum used to give me a game to play in my head when I was little and I couldn't sleep. 'Imagine the kind of tree-house you would build,' she'd say, 'if you were building a tree-house.' The effect was that I would stop worrying about not being able to sleep or whatever else was worrying me, and the next thing, I'd be asleep.

That's slightly different to what I'm talking about here but it's often the games we play as children that can plant the seeds for great ideas later in life. If I decided to become a psychologist, for example, like Shona but better, I might develop the *Eyes 1/Eyes 2* theory into a book that could prove useful for people with mental problems like depression.

In summary: looking at something while imagining you are looking at it, makes that thing okay. The wall is perfectly okay.

It's the same with dying.

I'm trying not to be bossy. Other kids find me annoying sometimes. I'm trying to explain about *Eyes 1* and *Eyes 2*. It's not even that hard. People don't always want to hear my theories, but this is the only theory I've got at the moment. I've been quite tired lately. High school is exhausting.

Something else I know is that people's teeth look a certain way when they are going to die from cancer. They get bigger and sort of milky and shiny. It's not just my dad. I've seen it with other people too. It's most tragic when you see those teeth in magazines and they say, the cancer is all gone and I'm getting on with my life. Because you can tell, just by their smile, that the cancer hasn't gone at all. My dad's teeth have had the milky look for months.

I put some ice chips against his lips because he likes that. He sees me. I know he sees me by the way he blinks. He's barely recognisable, to be honest. All puffy and swollen and dry. His hair grew back wavy, which is weird too.

Nurses put their heads around the open door every twenty to thirty minutes. I'm expecting Eleanor any second.

'Everyone okay in here, then?' she says, right on cue (twenty-seven minutes). I like her English accent. (You said to use dialogue, but not too much.) 'You call out if you need anything then, right?' I nod again. She's nice. I like her white dress and her soft shoes and the way her hair is smooth and the same every day. I wish all girls were like her. And like you, Mrs K.

My mother is a maths teacher so I know about some of the things that you go through. All those boring staff meetings. And the reports! Some teachers cut and paste the same four comments into every child's report. This is disrespectful and unprofessional, but sometimes you can only do what you can do.

You didn't cut and paste. You only gave me a C, but I know why. (It probably should have been a D.)

There's more dialogue. More of the rattly breathing first. It comes and goes; it's not something to be scared about.

'Is she in there? I want to see her. Why? Why can't I see ...?'

That's what he says, cracked and groggy.

I'll just put my laptop down for a minute.

I'm back. I put my hand on his. His hand was cold and felt like touching raw chicken. I said, 'It's okay, Dad. It's Martin here. You're in hospital. It's 11.05 Friday morning. It's May twentieth.'

They get disoriented, and you have to reassure them about where they are and what day it is.

I wouldn't mind if my mum and Aunty Pippa came back soon.

I eat the Violet Crumble.

More rattly breathing. His eyes flicker open and close and open and then close again. I watch him carefully: *Eyes 2*. I'm not saying it's easy.

I think about where people go when they die. I imagine what a spirit might feel like if you could touch it, which you can't. I think about how cremation is going to work. We're going to scatter his ashes at the top of Mt Lofty. I'm going to wear both of our karate belts when we do it.

You have to be careful that your thoughts don't get too close to the edge of your brain and fall off. Falling thoughts feel very similar to actually physically falling, but much scarier. Like jumping from a skyscraper with your eyes wide open. I imagine a skyscraper in Singapore, the biggest I've seen. (Dad vomited the whole way over, and Mum said we shouldn't have gone.) If you feel your thoughts getting too close to the edge, you have to pull them back. I sometimes think of myself as a cowboy (used to be Woody but now Clint Eastwood) and I lasso my thoughts back.

Shona and Mum say I've got Asperger's syndrome but my dad doesn't agree and neither do I. If labels are correct they can be useful, otherwise they are not. Also, I read the book on it and I don't tick all the boxes – some, yes, but not all.

In the 1990s everyone was diagnosing children with ADHD and putting them on Ritalin. Now it's Asperger's syndrome. Anyone that's not like everyone else – one of the popular kids – has Asperger's. It's as fickle as fashion. Also: 'opinions are like assholes; everybody's got one' (Clint Eastwood as Dirty Harry).

There's nothing wrong with Asperger's syndrome, don't get me wrong. I read *The Curious Incident of the Dog in the Night-Time* and I enjoyed it, I really did. Shona gave it to me after my dog went missing. We never found out what happened, so it wasn't the same. And I don't have Asperger's, like Shona said Christopher does. It's in my top five favourite books, though.

You're probably guessing, Mrs K; I'm struggling to find a complication. All the chocolate has made me feel a bit sick and it's quite hot in here. My dad is sleeping again. I've been watching his chest rising and falling – sometimes it stops in a rise and stays there for a while, hovering. And then it stops on the down and you wonder if it will take off again and you almost hope it won't. You want it to stop. You want the expectant feeling to stop. You hope that things might go back to the way they were, before this.

Mum and Aunty Pippa are back. They look like they've been running – their eyes are bright and wide and their faces are pink and when Mum puts her hand on my shoulder, it is very cold. Mum says I will go home soon with Aunty Pippa. I can come back after dinner. We're sort of doing shifts. Mum and Aunty Pippa are looking at each other back and forth, quickly, the way friends with a secret do.

Here is an example of why that is strange: last Christmas Aunty Pippa brought two pavlova rolls filled with kiwifruit and cream to our house for the tea-time dessert. She put them on the kitchen bench. I was sitting on a bar stool eating cherries, making a pyramid with the stones. My mum said, 'Phillipa, you filled them with kiwifruit.'

'Yes,' she said. 'Is there a problem?'

'I'm allergic to kiwifruit,' my mum said.

'Oh. I always forget which one it is,' my aunty said.

'It's only been fifteen years,' said my mum, and she said it quietly but angry, like a cat snarling.

A crisis, like someone dying, can bring people together. That's a cliché (which you said not to use) but also may be true.

Now Mum and Aunty Pippa are standing on either side of the bed. Aunty Pippa has put a hand over her mouth, like people do in movies. My mum has the tiniest smile and is shaking her head very slowly. Mrs K, this might be the climax of my narrative. Or even the resolution. My mum wants me to come over to the bed but I don't. She tells me to put my laptop down and come over but I won't. The closer you move in, the harder it is to do *Eyes 2*.

The horrible rattly breathing starts again. My mum sits down. Aunty Pippa smiles at my mum and puts her hand on my shoulder.

Everything dies, Mrs K. The orange tree in our backyard that's covered in oranges, one day that won't be there.

If it had happened today, Mrs K, I could have called this 'The Day My Dad Died', which possibly would have been an engaging title.

THE HONESTY WINDOW

A small printed card offered extra towels, if they should need them. They hadn't been provided in the first instance, Leah read, because the guesthouse was eco-friendly. The card was cream-coloured, expensive and embossed with an unfamiliar font. Leah rubbed the corner between thumb and forefinger, tilting her head to one side. Normally, she could pick card stock with her eyes closed. Oh well: she propped it back on the marble bathroom vanity, angled just so. In the mirror she caught a glimpse of her wrist tattoo, old and shabby, the black heart more blue smudge these days. She rotated her forearm back and forth, watching the tattoo appear and disappear in the mirror, like it belonged to someone else, someone a long way from here.

Leah was in the Barossa Valley, and this was the poshest guesthouse she'd ever seen. The only other time she was somewhere nearly as posh was their wedding night the year before. They were in the city then, at the Hilton. She remembered Patrick telling her that hotels say 'eco-friendly' because it's trendy, when really they can't be bothered washing your extra towels. He was standing in a pair of green satin boxers when he said that. She remembered watching his clean, pale body as she folded the second-hand wedding dress and laid it in the pearly cardboard box provided by the hotel. How sure Patrick had seemed then, how his eyes shone with certainty – about the towels, about all sorts of things.

He was asleep now. He lay stomach-down, one arm dangling over the side of the bed, his face slack, lips fuller than usual. Patrick looked different asleep: loose, even the texture of his skin. Watching him sleep made Leah uneasy, as if she might be called upon for something she wasn't capable of. When Patrick was a newborn baby, his mother had told her, he slept all day, and all she did was stare at him. 'Hours and hours,' his mother had said. 'And intuitively, I just did it intuitively. I didn't know anything about attachment theory back then.'

Shona had dropped in unexpectedly and seen the box of Pregnosis on their kitchen bench. Even though Leah and Patrick had said they weren't going to say anything until it had actually happened. It was an 'agreement'. So many agreements. Leah was left thinking: what the hell is attachment theory?

Getting pregnant was the reason they were here, but it didn't really make sense; the second MasterCard was for emergencies only. Patrick had said that, but then he used it to book them this suite. One night in this guesthouse was the same as a week's mortgage repayment. Plus, Leah could have got them something for under $100 on lastminute.com that still would have been nice. Not as nice as this, for sure. She picked up the miniature toiletries, one by one, put them back down again. They were so much prettier than their full-size versions. Just like real babies. They were Aveda, too. Expensive. Her mind wandered to eBay, as it did. With the insertion fees it was hardly worth it for something so small. If she had more, though, she could arrange them into gift packs, start them at 99 cents. They'd go off at 99 cents. Might finance an entrée in the restaurant, she thought ruefully, or one of those little chocolates with coffee. She slid her fingers down the smooth cabinetry and pushed – a gentle, satisfying *click*. She squatted to inspect the open cupboard: black hairdryer, single roll of toilet paper, a small pile of white paper bags. No stockpile of Aveda.

Leah stood and let her eyes wander 360 degrees. She hadn't properly taken it all in when they'd first arrived, just a quick glance around before Patrick pulled her to the bed. He'd used the word 'weighty' as he placed their bags into the alcove of the thick sandstone wall. 'Weighty' was a Shona word: odd – not one that people would normally use to describe a guesthouse. Patrick's mother was a psychologist and had lots of 'buzzwords'. Even still, Leah could see what Patrick meant: this place was weighty. The ensuite was total luxury: white and cream and chrome. The spa bath was deep and long, big enough for two people lying head to toe. Above it was a tiled recess lined with glass jars filled with pastel-coloured salts and other jars holding unlit tea lights. A chrome rail-thing lay across the bath and held a bar of handmade-looking soap. An oversized yellow rubber duck sat next to the soap. The duck was purposely out of place, Leah knew that. It was meant as a novelty, like that artist lady Shona always invited to her 'soirees': Tubby, Tabby, whatever her name was. Leah had casually asked how you spell 'soiree' and then typed it into her phone. *Why don't you just call it a 'barbie'?* she wanted to say to Shona. She undid the plush bathrobe she'd found on the bed and then pulled it in tighter round her waist. She didn't feel like having a bath anymore. She checked her new Fiorelli watch – had only just stopped feeling guilty whenever she looked at it – five-thirty. Another one and a half hours before dinner. She would wake Patrick in an hour, at the latest. They'd argued again till two this morning, the usual topics – sex (he said it was like she wasn't *there*), finances (why were they going somewhere so expensive if they couldn't even manage the mortgage?), her (he said 'anger issues').

The restaurant was part of the guesthouse, and sort of famous. It had been on *Postcards* on TV and also in the *SA Life* magazine she'd seen at the doctor's. The magazine said it could be hard to get a booking in the restaurant, that you had to be organised and plan ahead. She and Patrick had a booking at seven.

Sex was out of the way. It was feeling more and more like the article said it would. The article was like a self-fulfilling prophecy. *Keeping Your Sex Life Alive While Coping With Infertility* – it was by someone called Judith and she had a PhD about it. Judith said that sex was once spontaneous and fun and about passion and lust, but now it was more like a task and just about the calendar and when the woman was ovulating. Leah was ovulating now, that was certain – she could feel it: the pulling ache down one side of her pelvis. It wasn't as if they'd had any of the tests yet – it was still early days. 'You're both very young,' the GP told them, and she managed to smile and frown with the one expression. 'We'll try for another twelve months before we'll start worrying about anything.' She said 'we' as if she'd be trying too. It was Patrick's idea that they see the doctor. He'd thought they'd get pregnant the first time he didn't use a condom.

It was just like Patrick to find that article. And to organise this. To try and find solutions for problems that didn't even exist. 'Somewhere really special,' he'd said. 'It'll be romantic, even if it doesn't happen.'

When Patrick talked like that – sentimental – Leah twitched and squirmed like the baby guinea pig those kids brought over to show them after work last Friday. Those kids had no boundaries: they were always jumping the fence to show Leah and Patrick things – a gecko with no tail, new skateboards, boxes of fundraising chocolates – and the little one, the girl, she was too young to be jumping fences and visiting strangers' houses. Leah would know. You can have a hold of Cappuccino if you want to, the boy had said. Leah put her hands in her pockets, in case he forced the guinea pig on her. She was slightly repulsed by the rodent-like thing, but she felt sorry for it too, writhing away in the kids' hot small hands.

~

Leah worked at Joe Barnett's printing shop: out the back. She told people 'retail' but really she was out the back, stacking and packing orders. When people asked Patrick, and he said 'electrician' or 'sparky', Leah felt proud and annoyed. That was a proper job that needed a piece of paper. She'd left school at the end of Year 10, back when you still could – it was hardly a choice. If she had a chip on her shoulder for not finishing high school, the new night job at Coles wasn't helping.

Last week she'd seen Patrick's brother's new girlfriend in Aisle Four. Always 'Patrick's brother' when she thought of him now, never Scott. His girlfriend had described to Leah the shortfalls of the new beauty salon next door. It might be open after hours, she said, but it was irrelevant because they were hopeless and that was why she had the big red blotch between her eyebrows: they'd practically *burnt* her with the wax. She could sue, probably. Leah had kept stacking. She liked the part where you lined the tins into perfectly neat rows and she didn't really blame the girlfriend for going on – it wasn't as if she had a uniform or anything.

'Oh! What're you doing?' the girlfriend said, and only then did Leah remember her name: it was Jess. Patrick's brother had a new girlfriend every month.

'Working,' Leah said, 'I work here.' She laughed lightly.

'Oh. Oh! Sorry! I thought you worked at the printing place in the main street? Does Joe Barnett still own that?'

'Yeah.' Leah rolled her eyes. 'Mortgage.' She didn't say anything about trying for a baby. Jess nodded slowly, like she was doing quiet calculations.

Patrick's brother had a new franchise with Donut Delirium. Jess was the company's accountant and had helped with the start-up. Patrick's brother was always starting business ventures. 'The population up here is going off,' he told Leah, 'and you have to grab your market share.' Girlfriends were found wherever he went; the old were dumped, or he'd kid them up and try and keep two or more going at once. He found girls at The Barker, in cafes, down in the city at clubs, once on a football trip to Melbourne, a rodeo trip to Alice Springs, and once, half passed out on the street: that was Leah.

Leah was replaced by Kate, the American twice his age who he met in Cambodia. Leah fell harder than anyone expected. In the space of two weeks, she lost six kilos and it showed. Shona had stroked Leah's cheek, said perhaps she might like to stay for a bit, to get back on her feet.

'Sometimes I'm scared my brother is amoral,' Patrick said to her. 'I mean, that he has no conscience. That he doesn't even care about other people.' He'd taken Leah to Millie's, where he bought her a hot chocolate and a shiny custard tart. She felt him staring at her mouth while she ate. She'd seen parents of small kids lean forward like that, watching every mouthful for the satisfaction of those calories in.

~

Leah walked around the bed and quietly pushed the louvred doors dividing the two rooms of the suite. She let her fingers drag across the black marble top cut around the stainless steel sink. Everything in here felt like this: heavy, shiny, deep. The walls themselves would have to be a foot thick. Nothing was skimped, cut back or faked. Not like their house. They'd taken the cheapest option for everything and sometimes no option at all: no flywire on any of the screen doors and no floor covering in the spare room, just bare cement. It wasn't like she had imagined, not perfect, with everything neat and clean and

...ke the Harvey Norman catalogues.

... seemed so unbelievable in the beginning – an ...le fantasy – like pressing her face against the window ... ...nne Golding's dollhouse; that girl didn't know she was alive. The one afternoon Leah had spent at Deanne's house had been a revelation. She'd wanted to shrink herself. She'd wanted to sit on one of those little burgundy velvet couches with the turned mahogany legs in that tiny perfect lounge room with the real wallpaper on all the walls. Her skin had tingled at the back of her neck, like it always did when she wanted something badly. It travelled down her back, exactly the same, when she and Patrick drove around the new licorice-black streets of Gladeview Park estate.

Leah liked to chart the progress of other people's dreams. Up they went, frame by frame, brick by brick. Saturday afternoons she spent reading AV Jennings floor-plan pamphlets like they were romance novels. It was her biggest, most consuming desire, and the desire itself was soothing, a rush of calm, like a drug coursing through her veins.

Patrick worked double shifts – he'd sold his car to pay his brother's creditors, and there was the wedding too. And then, incredibly, Lot 39 was theirs. They had champagne with Shona and Patrick's brother and his new girlfriend, Bec, manager at the new Gloria Jean's on Morphett Street.

For months, Leah and Patrick went to the Lot alone, after work and on Saturdays and Sundays. They'd pick up McDonald's Meal Deals and have picnics there, play 'what room would I be in now in Blueprint 155 or Aurora 130?' games. They cancelled their Foxtel, stopped doing Friday nights at The Barker, moved in with Shona. What they were building would be real and solid. That was how they felt, even though the walls of their new home were only paper thin.

Leah pushed her knee into the wall of the guesthouse and felt its resistance against the side of her hip. You couldn't dent these walls. At home, they cracked and collapsed against the heel of your shoe. Six weeks in the new house and there it was, the first splintered gash in the plasterboard.

Leah wanted to say this: it wasn't a big deal. It looked worse than it was, than it should have been, than she'd *meant* it. And it wasn't as if she'd hurt a person: it was a *wall*. Patrick was all wide-eyed and quiet. It would have been so much more straightforward if he'd yelled back, maybe kicked something too. But the hole was in the lounge room, at the front of the house – they'd gone with the Aurora 130 – where everyone could see it.

And so Leah had agreed to see Jane.

'Perhaps,' Jane offered, after their third session of going nowhere, 'perhaps you feel … angry that … do you think, maybe you feel some jealousy … toward Patrick?'

Leah turned her head and looked Jane in the eye. Jealousy toward Patrick? She wondered then if Jane had talked to Shona. Wasn't there a privacy thing, even if Shona was paying?

'Because, you know, that would be very understandable, Leah. Very understandable, when I think about some of the things you've told me, some of the things you've told me about your own childhood … all that *chaos*?'

Jane was leaning in, sitting on the edge of her trendy yellow chair. Leah saw that a strand of her frizzy orange hair was stuck to the corner of her mouth. She tried very hard to imagine all that hair straight. Would it even be possible, Leah wondered, to use a straightener on hair as frizzy as that?

Chaos? Jane didn't know the half of it; nobody <u>did</u>.

'Okay, then,' Jane said, crossing one leg over the other and leaning even further in, 'what is it about Shona, do you think, that makes you *soooo* mad?' Jane growled and huffed through the word 'mad', as if Leah needed it acted out.

Had she said that Shona made her mad? She couldn't remember; maybe she had. She looked around the room trying to remember how they'd got to here – had she missed something? She'd been thinking about what she would put on Jane's desk, if it was her desk – certainly not that ugly ceramic elephant. Maybe an oversized hourglass, like the one in the gift shop that was always closing down.

'You love me, don't you, Leah?' She could barely look at Patrick when he'd said that. She'd been telling him about Jane's hair, about how orange and crazy and frizzy it was. Patrick often laughed at Leah's stories and impersonations. She thought he might find it funny, with her joke about Jane practically falling off her chair. They were pulling into the driveway. Those words came out of Patrick's mouth like they were spring-loaded.

'What?' Leah said, climbing out of the car, smoothing her jeans. 'What do you mean? Of course.'

Smith?

~

Leah heard rustling and a small groan from the bed. Patrick had turned his body, shifted the pillow under his head and pulled the waffled blanket over himself. His eyes were still

158

closed. It felt weird poking around the suite while he slept. She felt as if she was in a bubble, not really here, as though these moments didn't properly count for anything. She watched his bare shoulder roll faintly back and forth with his breath. Patrick had the same pale, freckled skin as his dad, something Leah had learnt from photos. Patrick's dad wasn't dead but he was as good as dead (Shona's words). He'd run off with Heather Schmidt – one of his parishioners – when the boys were teenagers. The two families had been close friends. Back then, it was church on Sundays, youth group on Fridays, camping trips, car-pooling to footy practice and tennis clinics – even Christmas dinners together. It wasn't something they chose, Patrick's dad had explained to his family; it wasn't about choice. He told them that he and Heather were soulmates and were moving to Byron Bay. When he didn't come to Patrick and Leah's wedding (too difficult for everyone), he'd sent a long letter instead. They were building a straw-bale house, Patrick's dad wrote, and it was nearly finished. Patrick and Leah were invited to come and stay. *We both can't wait to meet her*, the letter said. And the guest room, where they would sleep, had an 'honesty window', which meant they could look through it and see that the house really was made of straw. Patrick had laughed at that, hard and fast like a machine gun. Then he folded the letter over and over until it was a tiny square and tossed it in the drawer with his Duke of Ed certificates and old school reports. He'd barely seen his dad since he was sixteen, he told Leah.

Patrick was always meant to go to university. But then it was just about money and how to get it quickly. It was Shona who went in the end, starting with the STAT when the boys were finishing high school and then slogging away until she had an undergraduate science degree and then honours and then her proper psychology degree. Everything about his mum had changed, Patrick told Leah, even her hair and the way she dressed. My mum is amazing, Patrick told Leah.

The boys were still part of the youth group, still going to their dad's old church back when Leah first turned up, skinny and gothic and tied to nothing and no one. 'You, young lady, are staying for dinner,' Shona said when Scott brought her home like a stray mangy cat. Then Shona said, 'Lasagne!' like it was a big announcement, and she pulled a massive pyrex dish out of the oven like she was used to feeding football teams, as if she was the greatest woman who ever lived. Garlicky beef and burning cheese and smoky acidic tomatoes filled Leah's nose, and she realised she was starving but also nauseated and weirdly light-headed. Scott's hand resting inside her thigh under the table. Patrick watching her and his brother from the opposite side.

~

Leah knelt to open the bar fridge. It fit neatly inside a mahogany sideboard; custom made, no doubt. French champagne, a row of three whites, two cans each of tonic water and dry ginger ale, a block of Green & Black's organic dark chocolate, and a small stainless-steel carafe three-quarters filled with milk. She closed the door, stood up. Above the sideboard was a wall-mounted shelf holding two hardcover books on luxury ecological hotels

of the world. Next to these was a line-up of miniature bottles –
tiny spirits and liqueurs. She reached for the Belvedere Vodka.
Ran her thumb over the embossed white winter tree branches
wrapping the bottle. This wasn't shoplifting, because you
were *supposed* to help yourself to a mini-bar. But the impulse
felt familiar. Anyway, she'd cut back on that – just a few small
things – watches, bracelets, rings, and only when she was down
in the city. She never did it in Mount Barker and only did the
chains: Witchery, Sportsgirl, Diva, Dotti. Most of it she sold in
the evenings, on eBay, when Patrick was watching TV. It was
only keeping things that made her feel guilty.

She twisted the tiny black lid, split the paper label and
pulled out the miniature cork. Vodka hit the back of her throat
and spilt across her lips. She wiped her mouth with the back
of her hand, scraping her lower lip with the little metal prongs
on her engagement ring. She pressed a palm to her lip and laid
the empty bottle at the bottom of the small black bin, carefully
covering it with a tourist brochure. She reached for the mini
single-malt whisky, split the foil lid and drank that too. Then
the Bombay Sapphire gin in its pretty turquoise bottle. The
Cointreau rolled sickly sweet in her mouth and burnt the back
of her throat.

She tried to remember how last night's arguing had started,
but all the words – his and hers – seemed grainy, blurred,
like they had no meanings. She tried to bring them forward
for close inspection, tried to remember why she was trying.
This was how she felt when Jane did the hypnosis. Jane said
hypnotherapy could be very useful with memory trauma,
though she didn't use it with everybody. Jane wanted Leah to

relive the whole thing with her mum and the boyfriend with the Kawasaki 250, from when she was five and they were at the river. She still had the burn scar, mottled and sloppy, like she'd spilt her own skin down her ankle.

Jane wanted Leah to *talk* to her five-year-old self, to comfort and reassure her, to tell her that she was safe now, that she could leave all that hurt – all that *chaos* – behind. Over and over Jane droned on: *all is well, all is well.* Leah lay back in the recliner like Jane said, closed her eyes even, breathed in that slow, measured way. She imagined stacking tins of tuna and cans of chopped tomatoes and boxes of Barbecue Shapes. It was like one of those old-fashioned video games, and she had to stop them crashing down, *blip-blip-blip*, as she stacked.

When Jane asked in that flat, funny voice she was using for the hypnosis, 'Can you see her, Leah?'

Leah had whispered, 'Yup.'

'Why don't you hold her hand?' Jane had suggested then.

What? Leah thought: I don't want to hold her stupid hand.

'Okay,' she'd said, clearing her throat, and Jane whispered: 'Great.'

~

Leah rolled her tongue across her lip, a lick of blood and the beginnings of a blister. She pressed her finger into the puffy rise and then moved her hand away, stretching it in front of her. Her fingers were long and fine – 'Piano hands!' Shona had declared on that first night, clutching them in her own and giving them a squeeze.

Leah wriggled her fingers, as if she were playing piano midair. Her engagement ring and wedding band swung around, still too loose, even though they'd been refitted twice now.

Patrick had bought the diamond ring without her knowing – without anyone knowing – secretly had put it on lay-by at Shiels and paid it off slowly.

One night in the middle of summer, Patrick took her to a Thai restaurant down in the city (Leah had never eaten lemongrass and he couldn't believe it). On the way back up the freeway he'd turned off at Eagle on the Hill. The air was still, as though a breeze had never blown and never would again. She was wearing a floral dress with a girlish bow tied at the back, found at the op shop and not really her style. Her thighs were sticky with sweat, her stomach bloated from all the rice.

And then Patrick was kneeling in front of her, one knee up, like in fairy stories and movies. 'Leah,' he said, and he pulled the red velvet jewellery box from his jeans pocket. Later she realised he must have had it there all night. All through her talking about moving to Darwin and the things she said about Scott. 'I can make you happy,' Patrick told her. 'You should marry me.' He opened the box, took out the ring and said it again: 'I can make you happy.' Then he slid it onto her finger, where the diamond swung around and hung loosely out of sight. 'We can get it resized!' He laughed, as if he'd solved the only thing that would ever stand in their way.

She wanted to slow everything down. She wanted to catch up. She wanted to say: *Wait! I don't feel well. I don't like this dress. It's too hot. My mascara is all smudged.*

She kissed him.

And then Patrick became all serious. 'Leah, I believe something,' he said. He held her face in his hands. 'I believe that we're *meant* to be together. We're *meant* to get married.'

She nodded, lowered her brow and said, 'Yeah.'

The effect was like a line of dominoes falling. For a moment she was quiet, transfixed by the notions assembling in her mind. 'Imagine ...' she said, and she looked into his shining eyes, beads of sweat pooling in their corners. 'Imagine ...' she said again, '... if I'd never left Sydney? If I'd never come up here that night, no idea where I was? Patrick, you know I had no idea where I was! Imagine if your brother hadn't seen me at the bus stop? Imagine if I'd never stayed, never gone to the youth group? Imagine if you'd stayed home that Friday night? If you hadn't played that game of footy? If you'd still been on crutches? Imagine if none of those things had happened?' And she laughed, incredulous, amazed.

Scott's new girlfriend – Kate – and that stupid holiday in Cambodia, were suddenly, strangely irrelevant. All the other girls too. Then and there, Scott became 'Patrick's brother'.

Leah could still recall the fleet of expressions that passed over Shona's face when they got home and announced the news and presented Leah's new ring. Patrick's mother turned Leah's hand in hers, and stared hard at the diamond as it slid around, back and forth like it was a small but dangerous creature that had made its way into her home. Very softly, her voice strange and high at the end, she said, '*Patrick.*'

~

Leah turned away from the sideboard and the fridge and the shelf and leant across the small breakfast table, toward the covered window. The man in Curtains and Blinds had demonstrated raising a Roman blind when they'd gone in for a quote last year.

'There's no point, then, is there?' Patrick had said after they'd moved into their new house. 'No point in saving for that blind.' It was a question, but his voice was pleading.

'What d'you think?' Leah had shot back. 'Jeez, Patrick, they were just shitty old sheets. I wouldn't have done it if we had the new blind. As if I would've ripped a new blind.' Part of her believed it. She did lose her shit sometimes, it was true, and she wasn't proud of it, but it was never at people. And apart from the hole in the lounge room wall, the only other holes were in the wall of their walk-in robe, not in any public space. Not anywhere people could see.

So they still had ugly old sheets tacked over all their windows. In winter, it would be freezing.

She angled and pulled the cord on the Roman blind and wound its slack around the bird-shaped chrome hook. Her mouth pushed against a smile. It had to be the prettiest time to come to the Barossa Valley. Row after row of shiraz vines, some with leaves still in faded green, others deep red or burnt orange, others completely naked, with dark, knotted limbs. Streaks of sunlight cut through the vines and the grey of the cool afternoon. Small brown sparrows hopped and dipped through leaves littering the ground. The perfect place to make a baby. Beautiful Patrick was right, absolutely right. Coming here was an excellent idea. She wondered why she'd questioned it. Because being here did make sense. The skin around her cheekbones slackened, her shoulders dropped in that familiar and lovely way. Her breath was slow and relaxed. She had a thought about alcohol but it was vague. Was it something she'd discussed with Patrick? Jane? Or maybe it was both?

No, that's right. She remembered. You weren't supposed to drink alcohol when you were pregnant or trying to be pregnant. Or was it only when you were actually pregnant? She checked her watch. And that. She would stop. The shoplifting was just a little habit, like those women who ate too many carbs and those men who looked at too much porn. Something she could control, absolutely.

She made her way to the bed where Patrick was sleeping. She lay down next to him and pushed her face into the back of his neck. He groaned and reached a hand behind him, placed it across the back of her thigh and gently squeezed. 'Hey, baby,' she said.

He flipped his body over so that his face was close to hers. 'Hey, yourself.' He pulled her in closer and she giggled and then lifted her head and found his mouth with her tongue, warm and sour.

He pushed her back to the length of his pale, freckled arm. She ran her hand back and forth across his bicep, arched her neck.

He grabbed her hand still and held it up high. Awake now, he propped on his elbow. 'Leah! Really? Spirits? Fuck.' He flung himself back down on the bed, ran a hand through his hair and then covered his face.

She didn't want him to be sad or cross. She smiled. Yes, she'd been drinking. She was probably drunk. But it felt good.

He should see the view from their window. She moved her hands over his chest and hooked her foot over his ankle.

'Leah, please. What are you doing? How long have I been asleep? An hour? I thought you were going to have a bath. You said you were going to have a bath. We were ... Don't you want ...?' He made a sound as though he were trying to lift something beyond his strength. He pushed her away and sat up on the bed with his head in his hands. He stayed like that for a long moment, and she worried that he might be crying. She hated it when Patrick cried. Then he stood quickly, walked into the ensuite. She heard his feet padding around on the marble tiles. She heard him say, 'God. We had an agreement.'

She sat up on the bed. Tucked her hands under her thighs.

Patrick reappeared in the doorway. 'Leah.' He often did that: said her name at the beginning of sentences, like people did with children. 'This has got ...' He ran a hand roughly over his face. 'This stuff has got to end. I can't keep doing this. Feeling like I'm living in a ... I dunno. I don't know. I don't even know. What you're going to do next.' His eyebrows were bunched, his teeth chewed his bottom lip. 'Leah,' he said again, and this time his voice broke on it. 'I need to know if ...' He gulped for air, his pale, freckled chest puffing and then deflating.

'Patrick, I just had a couple of drinks. S'fine. You should have one too. You need to relax.' She pushed herself back onto the bed and circled her stomach with her hands. Imagine if there was a baby in there now. Imagine if an egg had met a sperm and their cells were multiplying together right now, forming an embryo, a zygotey thingamajig ...

right now, as she lay on this bed. Imagine what they would tell everyone. A baby. She wanted to say this to Patrick, to paint a picture of this possibility, to cheer him up. She heard him slap the doorframe with his palm. Then he knocked his head against the wall.

He said her name again. 'I need to know if you love me, Leah. If you want to be with me. Please. Just tell me if you love me. You never say it, Leah.'

This again. It always came back to this. She sat up. 'I do. I do say it, Patrick. God.'

He raised his arms, hooked them over the frame of the doorway and shook his head in disbelief, a small, sad smile across his lips.

'Okay. I love you. Alright?'

'I need to know how you love me.'

'Huh?'

'How do you love me?' His voice was urgent.

'I don't know what you mean. I don't know what you mean, Patrick.' She felt her forehead tighten above her eyes.

'How? Please. You said you love me. But how do you love me? Like a friend? Like a brother? Like a father?' He slammed the palm of his hand against the doorframe again. 'Just say it. Say it. I need to know.'

'Patrick. Calm down. I had a couple of drinks. It's not that bad. Shit. I thought we were supposed to be relaxing. Making a baby, whatever. I thought this was what this ... was all supposed to be. Arghhh!' She put her hands through her hair. It felt thin and greasy, and she remembered vaguely that she was going to wash it in the bath.

'I need to know, Leah: *how* do you love me?' His jaw was clenched. His eyes dark and strangely wide.

Leah felt sick. 'Alright! Okay, okay.' She thought she might vomit. 'I love you like ...' She searched herself. She realised that it was like something. She stood, swayed slightly, felt the robe loosen and fall off her left shoulder.

If she hadn't drunk the spirits, she'd probably be able to think of what it was, how she loved Patrick, work this out. Because she did love him. But something had been buzzing in the back of her mind since she saw that rubber duck sitting on the bath in the ensuite. Something she'd forgotten, from a long time ago. A specific, little memory. Somehow it seemed relevant to this very important question that needed an answer, though she wasn't sure how.

She'd been alone. Had she thought to call the police? Unlikely. But she was too little to be alone. She must have called the police. Well, someone did. Was she seven? Eight? They'd come and picked her up. She sat in the back of the police car, and they drove in the dark across the city. She'd watched the lights blur into one straight neon line of red and blue, green and white. It must have been emergency foster care, just one night. There were a few of them, nights like that, but only once to this woman's house. Her name was Jean and she didn't have a husband, but she did have a glass-fronted cabinet filled with tiny dolls from all around the world. Her husband used to collect them for her, before he 'passed', Jean said. She let Leah touch them. Dolls in kimonos, in German dancing dresses with their hair in perfect plaits, hair in sleek buns with blunt black fringes.

She stroked them and turned them in her hands and lined them up and rearranged them.

Then Jean had run her a bath. The bath was deep and pale pink. The tiles on the walls and floor were shiny black and the whole room was huge, bigger than any bathroom Leah had ever seen before. She sat up in the bath, straight backed, her thin hair tickling her dry shoulders. There was a rubber duck in that bath, probably put there as a toy for kids like her. Leah had watched it bob around her with its black beady eyes and its cold plastic body and she'd thought: *Orphan*. Being in that big bathroom naked and all alone with that rubber duck had somehow made her feel like an orphan. But not in an entirely bad way. The thought had given her a shiver and for a moment made her feel dramatic and curious. It was a strange mix of feelings.

Jane would love that.

Leah focused her eyes and saw that Patrick had clenched his hand into a tight fist. He slammed it into the doorframe, hard. It made a loud *whump*, a sickening crunch, like a small bird hitting a window. He pulled his fist back and pushed it hard into his forehead. Blood trickled through the cracks between his fingers, down to his head and across the length of his eyebrow. He pursed his lips, blinking furiously as the blood reached his eye.

'Like my Grade Four teacher.'

Patrick groaned. 'What?'

'Patrick. I loved my Grade Four teacher. He was my hero. He taught me everything about the solar system.' She flung her arms wide to demonstrate the hugeness of the solar system.

'Jesus.'

Patrick slid down the doorframe, squatting in his boxer shorts, his hand holding his head, clutching at his ginger hair. He leant back into the ensuite and reached for a handtowel, wrapping it thickly around his fingers.

Leah slunk to the floor next to him. He dropped down, let his legs flop loosely out in front, rested his head on the doorframe and closed his eyes. Leah picked up his bound hand and unravelled the towel. The fine hairs on his fingers were matted in blood, the white skin across his knuckles split and jagged.

'Oh, Patrick. Look what you've done,' she crooned. She turned over his hand. 'Look, it's okay, okay? Trust me.' She lifted his chin, and he opened his eyes, squinting as though he were looking into a bright light. 'Look what you've done,' she said again, and she shook her head back and forth and clicked her tongue. She moved his hand – limp and unresisting – across her body and placed it on her lower belly. Fresh blood from his knuckles streaked across the velvety white bathrobe. 'Look. We're going to have a baby, Patrick. A baby.' She spoke slowly and firmly, as though Patrick might be waking from a deep sleep. Leah held his hand on her stomach and looked into his face. 'You still don't get it, do you? I honestly loved my Grade Four teacher, Patrick.'

She rocked forward and arched her head around the corner to the kitchenette. The window was almost black now, the vines barely visible. Without the playfulness of light, they were just shadowy outlines, their branches menacing limbs. She leant back against the wall, Patrick's arm secured across her body with her elbow, his hand still resting across her belly.

His head was angled awkwardly against the doorframe, his eyes were closed again, his breath slow and shallow. Then he cupped his hand and gripped the hollow at her waist. He lifted his other arm wedged behind her back and wrapped it round her shoulders. He pulled her into his chest and buried his face into the top of her head. She felt his lips on her scalp.

Leah held the Fiorelli watch up to her face. It was well past seven. They'd missed their booking. They wouldn't be having tea in the famous restaurant. They would stay here in this room then, just the two of them. She wasn't hungry anyway. She snuggled back into Patrick's warm body. She felt the thumping of his heart against her shoulderblades, felt it begin to slow and then, a little later, she noticed that it matched exactly the gentle measured beating of her own heart.

WHAT I WISHED

I watch my three items slide along the conveyer belt. Milk, white bread, miniature muffins. A year and a half ago we were a normal family doing one big supermarket shop on Saturdays. Now I'm like one of those old ladies who buy only what they can afford in coins and carry in one bag, old ladies whose days stretch out before them in slow minutes, whose nights are long and lonely. I push the muffins closer to the bread and feel the conveyer belt vibrate under my hand, its hum grates into my ears. I just want to get back home. The supermarket is so loud. Everything beeps; there's so much beeping. We don't buy shaving cream anymore, or that anti-dandruff shampoo you liked to use. Other things I didn't even realise were peculiar to you: peanut butter, the orange pekoe teabags, those little biscuits with the white cream in the middle – we don't buy those now either. Everything was fast, maybe I didn't notice things back then. The girl on the checkout asks me how I am today, and I tell her I wish this rain would stop. She looks too young to be working at 9.15 on the morning of a school day. I look past her head through the window to the dreary grey outside. 'I wish the sun would start shining,' I tell her.

'Ah-ha. Be careful what you wish for.' This comes from the woman behind me, in one of those singsong voices certain women have. I've seen her in this supermarket before. I've seen her driving around town too. I don't know her, but still, the buzzing starts up in my chest; God, I wish this would stop. I bring my hand up to my neck and run my fingers back and forth across my collarbone. It makes no real sense, but I've found this small movement helps. Sometimes I do it at night when I can't sleep. It's not logical. Be careful what you wish for. She doesn't even know me.

'That's right,' the girl says. A small and silly-looking bandaid covers one side of her nose. 'When the rain stops,' she says, 'it'll be fire season before you know it. And hot, because I hate it when it's hot.' The girl and the woman look at each other as if they know the secret to a magic trick.

'Well, it's not just that,' the woman says. She's bent over unloading her things from the trolley and scrolling on her mobile. I used to multi-task like that. 'It wasn't that long ago that we were in a drought,' she says. 'Rain is good. People forget that rain is actually good. We need as much as we can get in this country.'

She's wearing a long hand-knitted jumper that comes down to her knees. I stare at her purchases stacked up and ready to be scanned. Soy milk and rice milk and gluten free and organic this and that. The front of her trolley digs into my hip as I'm trying to gather up my things. They don't give you bags anymore. You bring your own or you have to carry your purchases in your arms so that everyone can see them. Even as I walk through the electronic sliding doors and into the drizzling rain again, I can still hear all the beeping. A woman in the carpark is thrusting her trolley back and forth trying to unlock its jammed-up wheels, and I have to wait for her to finish before I can get to my car. Then I have to wait several long seconds before she realises I can't back out until she moves.

Three times on the way home I am signalled by men in orange vests holding *Slow* and *Stop* signs, and all around me jackhammers vibrate and hack into asphalt. It seems every road in town is being resurfaced. The Council does nothing and then everything all at once. You always said this road needs attention, how there needs to be a roundabout here and traffic lights there or some sort of chicane. Well, now they are doing it all – all at once. Some days it feels as though the whole town is detoured. And they take so long to clean up their mess; even when the works are complete the roadside is piled with detritus like a beach after high tide – all those ugly indecipherable things the ocean discards and leaves behind in piles to rot in the sun.

I stop at the letterbox at the top of our driveway to collect the mail. I try to avoid our neighbour. I'm sure she watches me through her curtains whenever I walk up to our letterbox. I guess you can't insure against loneliness. There's a pile of junk catalogues and a letter from the insurance company. My latest cheque.

'Are you okay?' The other mums still ask me this. They draw out 'okay' and drop their chins and give me meaningful looks. It's partly why I never went back to Curves. What they really want is gossip. They want to know if you had life insurance. They want to know how long I'm going to be able to live like this – not working – before the money runs out. They want to know whether I'll have to sell the house and transfer our son to Mount Barker High.

All those discussions we had about schools. I've been trying to remember all the things you said. You had opinions about this; I remember that.

The money came through. I traded in the Subaru, bought a new Pajero. We no longer have a mortgage. If I decide to sell, it won't be out of financial distress. What these women don't realise is how administrative it all is, how mundane. Stacks of paperwork lying around the house, things you don't know what to do with. I crammed myself with the anaesthetising fine print. This was how I discovered all the insurance possibilities. Accidental damage is entirely underrated. It isn't only about major disasters, about floods and bushfires and lightning strikes and tsunamis. Sometimes it's just the small things. Sometimes it's just little mishaps of life: losing things, forgetting things, dropping them absentmindedly onto your tiled floor where they smash into tiny shards that will ring in your ears for long minutes afterwards, long after you've cleaned all those pieces up.

So far I've received payments for my lost prescription sunglasses, the cracked shower screen, Martin's misplaced retainer (we found it afterwards) and, now, a $300 cheque for my grandmother's Wedgwood vase. I'm not saying there isn't a small amount of work involved. To prove ownership, I had to scan a photograph of the vase and email it to Josh in Small

Claims. I spent till two on Wednesday morning searching through the family photo albums. They stop in 2001 when we purchased the digital camera, even though we said we'd still print photos. Evidence of Martin's entire childhood exists inside the desktop. All those awkward birthday parties I insisted he have, the Lego castles he built and rebuilt, his feet tucked up under his bottom. All the discussions about what was best. 'Let him go,' you always said. 'Let him go.'

(I am, I think. I'm trying.)

I felt like a masochist looking through those albums. My chin kept spasming and more than once I had to press my fist hard at the base of my nose. I still don't understand crying. Let it all out, people say. Let it go. Or as that child posing as a hospital chaplain told me: Let go and let God.

I have no idea what he meant.

The photo I settled on was of you sitting in your chair with Martin as a newborn tucked into your elbow and draped across your forearm. The plastic Christmas tree was next to you, lights on, tinsel, baubles, the vase on the shelf just above your head. So I emailed that to Josh and now here I am, two days later with this, a cheque for $300. Just like that.

I put the milk in the fridge and hold the pale yellow cheque up to the light. In a universal sense, three hundred dollars isn't fair and it isn't justice. But it's a small stab at it, a lame punch to an oversized bicep. It keeps me occupied, anyway.

I take the smallest saucepan from the cupboard, fill it with water and put it on the cooktop on high. Gently lower in an egg. Two breakfasts has become a routine; one before I drop Martin to school and one when I get home again, often after a small errand. Yesterday morning I went to the GP. She prodded away at my back and shoulders – of course she did, her specialty is muscular-skeletal. 'Does it hurt here?' she asked. 'What about here? And here?'

'Look,' I told her, 'it hurts everywhere you touch. I'm really just here for the sleeping tablets.'

Grief manifests in all sorts of ways, she said. Apparently, you have to keep tabs on it, monitor it. I suppose she thinks I'm depressed. She gave me a brochure. It said that people often lost weight when they were grieving. There was no mention in the brochure of people putting *on* weight. Yes, I told her, I agree; grief isn't just about loss, the gaping hole in your life. It can be more complex than that. I considered telling her about the buzzing in my chest, the hive of bees that come and go, swarming in there like it's a hollow log. And then the sharp sting that comes out of nowhere, the slightest thing and then *jab*. I didn't say anything. I know what it is. My whole body aches with it. At night, my calves and hands and shoulders ache. In the morning, my teeth ache.

I said no to the lunch with Yolanda. People are still asking me to do things. You should do this; you should go there; come here with us. People always want something to *happen*. But the smallest thing feels like too much.

All I want to do is sit in your chair and stare, try to calm this constant static inside my head. I look around sometimes and I see our house as a stranger might, or a ghost, as if no one is in it, as if I am not in it. Perhaps I'm developing an imagination after all. If it feels like this, I don't want one.

You think that if no one is in your home there is nothing

happening in it. This is not true. Silence doesn't exist. There are things that buzz and bang, crackle and hum. Crickets, frogs, birds, barking dogs, tiny toes of rats, expansion of wood and metal and shrinkage of copper, rain on the roof like the distorted applause of a huge crowd. And all the variables of the wind as it comes and goes: whispering, chatting, changing its mind, working up a fury. All these things were happening in our home during those hours and hours, over all those years, when we weren't in it. All those hours I was running around teaching algebra and marking exams, collecting speeding fines and small bruises. While I was spinning webs and alibis as if I was the most creative left-brained person who ever lived. While I was achieving nothing on one of those stupid weights machines at Curves. Those women at Curves always talk about feeling guilty. Guilty for eating too much cake or not volunteering at the school canteen or doing enough exercise. The last time I went to Curves was before the second hospital trip last year. Thinking about the gym makes me tired now. Now I just sit here until it's time to pick Martin up from school, right on three. I suppose I am finally like one of those proper 'stay-at-home mums'. Still don't bake, though.

Other times I get up and wander from room to room, just looking around. Martin cut out the two death notices from the *Advertiser* and put them on his bedroom pin board. Today I see that they have started to curl a little at their edges. I often come in here and stare at them. And I try to imagine the notices becoming yellow and brittle like old newspaper does. But do you know, I can't do it. I can only watch it happen, slowly, in real time. I remember when I came home from that staff training day meant to encourage more creative teaching techniques, and I asked you if you could imagine a pink elephant with purple spots.

'I suppose,' you said. 'What's next?'

'You can picture that? Right now, out of nowhere, in your head? A pink elephant with purple spots?' I couldn't believe anyone could do it, least of all you, and as nonchalantly as that. I didn't understand what it even meant. Was there a picture in your brain as if you were looking at it on a piece of paper or on a television screen? People could do that? I felt in awe and intolerant, like I do of people who write poetry, and people who talk about their 'journey'.

Eric couldn't do it. He wasn't head of the whole math department then but he was on his way. He raised his eyebrows at me across the staffroom, which I read as: you and me, we're the same, we don't need this. When we walked out of the room that day, he cupped my elbow with his hand, as if he were guiding me somewhere.

'With practice,' the facilitator told us, 'any one of you can learn to do this, to use your right brain like this.' His name was Joseph, and I remember he wore a pink and purple striped shirt, as if that somehow proved it.

The thing that frightens me is this: I don't know what I believe about life and death. I cannot imagine life after death, so does that mean that it doesn't exist, or just that the right side of my brain doesn't exist? How can I know if there is more to it all, to this life, if I am dulled and blinded by the limitations of my own brain? Or is my lack of imagination evidence in itself that things such as heaven and angels are entirely subjective? I've always been quite pleased with my brain.

I want to know if you can hear me.

~

The saucepan is hissing in the kitchen, and I remember the egg.

I can't seem to make my legs move fast enough. I suppose it's the part of me that doesn't even care. I lift the saucepan off the hotplate. There are dark grey spots on the base, only a tiny bit of water left. I put the pan on the bench so I can get a spoon to rescue the egg. I guess it's hard-boiled, then. I've been doing all sorts lately. Not from rushing; not from moving at my usual pace, bumping my hips and elbows against doorframes and classroom desks. If anything, I am going too slowly, like those old people who cause car accidents from driving at a snail's pace. Everything has slowed down. Just a drop in to the supermarket or an appointment with the GP – a walk around the house – have become major excursions. Time and space can open right up and swallow you. Truly.

There is an acrid smell of burning plastic. I look down at the bench and realise that the laminex is melting under the saucepan. I lift it up again and put it in the sink, douse it with cold water. What was I thinking? Stupid. I leave the egg and inspect the benchtop. There is a section about the size of a fifty-cent piece: a small, blackened crater charred at the edges. You can see the cheap brown chipboard underneath. I wet some paper towel and clamp it over the burn, then I run my finger across it.

~

I have Josh from the insurance company on speed-dial. I am fond of him, the sound of his voice. Something unfettered and unburdened about him.

'Was there a flame?' he asks.

'Well, there wasn't *not* a flame,' I say. I am leaning over the sink. I can feel my lips grazing the mouthpiece. Josh is silent, waiting. Obviously he's learnt the art of not filling conversational gaps, but I can hear his breath, the strike of keys on his keyboard, the shuffling of paper.

'I didn't see a flame,' I offer, 'but I don't suppose that necessarily means that there wasn't a flame underneath, as I lifted the saucepan, that I didn't actually see.'

'Like I said,' Josh says, 'there really had to have been a flame. Otherwise it can't come under "Fire".'

Logic. I appreciate it. I run my fingers across the melted laminex again. I can cover it up easily enough with the salt pig, I suppose. Or I could leave it exposed. It could serve as a small reminder that bad things happen to good people, that you are not always in control, that shit happens, that ... wait for it ... life is like a box of chocolates. Yes, someone actually said that to me. At your funeral.

~

I finished it on a piece of grid paper, like it was a stupid schoolyard romance. I slipped it under Eric's hand and into his black leather diary. I wrote *my husband has inoperable cancer* and *this has to end*. Later, in the carpark at the end of the day, he held up my crumpled note and said, 'Good-o.' Then he swayed his head like a pendulum, as if he were weighing something, as if he were saying, *You win some, you lose some*. 'Sorry to hear about your husband,' he said, as if you'd missed out on a promotion at work. The moment he got into his car – the sports car you have when you're not having a sports car – the moment I saw the back of his head as he drove away, right at that moment, I felt nothing for him. Nothing.

~

When I picked up your hand from the bed on Saturday the twenty-first – you only had three more days – and I said, 'Darling,' that word felt foreign in my mouth. I hadn't called you that in years. I said it again and I stroked the back of your hand. It was pearly, almost translucent. Your legs looked like sticks under the covers. I'd left it too long. I knew it, but it seemed imperative.

'There's something,' I said, 'there's something I need to tell you.'

Your eyes opened and you looked straight at me. They were large and inky, so darkly blue that they were almost black. You lifted your index finger up from where it was resting in my hand and you held it there, and you kept your eyes on mine. Then you slowly lowered your finger. In that one tiny gesture, in that one single moment, knowing that any second Pippa or Martin would be back from the cafeteria, it had seemed so acutely clear what you were saying to me. I thought you meant to silence me. I thought you were saying: *I know*. I thought you were saying that you forgave me. The whole room seemed to be saying it.

But now I don't know. Now I'm not sure. I think maybe I made all that up. That I *imagined* it.

I want to know this: would you have left me?

What if people could take out infidelity insurance? So if you wanted to leave me, infidelity insurance would pay for your rent, your legal fees, your new white goods. There'd be cover for counselling. You could have claimed for the cost of a life coach and rebuilt your shattered ego.

Or maybe you didn't care.

Did you know that we are insured for falling debris from space? And against riot and civil commotion?

I didn't tell you everything. I barely told you anything. There's more.

~

It's impossible to judge how long it will take to get to the school at pick-up time with these roadworks, and I arrive too early. I take the car park closest to the reception building and sit with the window down. The rain has stopped and now there is a faint smell of sewage and eucalyptus, though it is not unpleasant. Through the side mirror, I see Martin walking toward the car. He has grown taller in these past months, lanky, like you, but stooped. He walks alone. All the other kids walk in clusters that contract and expand as they move. He disappears from my mirror and then the front passenger door opens and he throws his bag onto the floor and gets in after it.

'Hello,' I say.

'Hi. Go, please.'

'Are you okay, Martin?' I pull my hand away from the ignition and reach over to touch his shoulder, to look at him more closely. He flinches from me, his whole body prickling.

'I'm fine, Mum. Just go, please.' He makes small movements with his head from side to side, his eyes darting left and right. 'You don't need to come into the carpark anymore, you know. Just pick me up down the road. Can you go, please.'

I start the ignition and reverse the car out as quickly as I can. I want to get away from here too. I want to get away from all these kids and their matching school shoes and snarled expressions. I want to get away from everything that is public. Away from cars and people and jackhammers and shops and cafes and stupid men in orange vests with *Stop* signs in their grubby hands. I want to be done with the long afternoon and evening ahead, of making dinner and then cleaning it up. I want this day and everything in it to end. I want the darkness, the halfway respite that comes with night and sleep, when everything that torments me will settle into my jaw and leave the rest of me alone.

~

But later, sleep doesn't come. I lie awake feeling terrible. My skin feels itchy and hot, and I kick the quilt off, but then I get cold and pull it back up. Over and over like this.

I keep hearing the woman in the supermarket.

I know the exact day and time. It was 9 October last year.

Just before the cancer. I looked at the clock radio on Eric's bedside table in his Angas Street unit. It was 5.47pm. I was flushed, catching my breath. Everything made perfect sense, even the pale orange light of late afternoon as it landed on the corner of the bedspread. I felt as though I was on the cusp of something. I watched Eric, who was standing at the window looking down to the street. To be honest, I felt like I was a movie star, someone far more glamorous than me. I felt outside of myself, better than myself. I'd never felt like that before: conscious, more awake than awake. Then I looked at the red lights on the clock again, and I saw it change to 5.48. I saw that minute disappear, and I thought, What now? What happens now? That minute is gone. And then I thought of the long drive out of the city and up the freeway. I thought of all the clothes that would probably still be on the line, getting wet all over again. I remembered that it was tuna pasta night. I knew that I would probably have to make it. Then there'd be dishes. I closed my eyes, and it popped into my head. It had no weight or dimension. It just appeared. I had no desire to speak it out loud. It was a thought that came of its own accord, like the first raindrop that falls from an unsuspecting sky.

I wished you were dead.

~

I must have fallen asleep. I am woken by something electronic, a persistent beeping sound. All this beeping. I lie in bed listening, unsure whether the sound is being generated from inside or outside the house. It is probably the batteries in the kitchen smoke alarm. I sit up in bed, my face against the black night. I pull the quilt back from my body and rest it bunched together on your empty side. It is still strange, all this space to myself. I am not used to it. And I am not used to being completely in charge. I always thought I did everything: got up to Martin when he was a baby, researched the paediatricians and the psychologists, organised finances, called tradesmen, checked out strange noises in the night. But it isn't true. Now that I really am alone, now that I really am doing everything, I realise that it isn't true. Not at all. It weighs heavily; not just the knowledge that I hadn't done everything, but that now I do, and will.

I roll my body over the bed and stand, steady myself with a hand to the bedside table. I walk down the hallway, the tendons in my calves and ankles snagging and sore. The kitchen oven blinks 04.07. The beeping isn't coming from here, but I can still hear it, dulled now. I peer into the black of the kitchen window, see only my dishevelled self, limbs of trees outlined behind me. Perhaps it is someone else's smoke alarm from down the road or across the valley. Maybe a truck reversing on Springs Road. Who knows? I don't suppose it matters. It is only a leftover sound now, another one to tolerate in the background.

I make my way back down the hallway, trailing a hand along the wall to guide me. I won't turn on a light. Martin is an even lighter sleeper now. I stop at his open bedroom door and listen to his breathing for a while and then slowly walk back to my room.

After the ruffling sounds of rearranging the quilt and settling my body back down on the mattress and my head on the pillow, I realise that the beeping has stopped completely.

Whatever it was, it is nothing now. But I am fully awake. I lie quietly, listening. A frog starts up, like a miniature toy machine gun. Another joins in and then nothing. An early magpie warbles, another frog and then nothing. I lie motionless, listening, straining for what else I can hear out there, but there really is nothing now. What follows is a long stretch of silence that wraps around me. It is so long there is nothing left to measure time against. It is silence with texture – velvety and thick – and I wonder if this is true silence.

I whisper your name into it. The silence seems to take my utterance and digest it whole. There is no trace of your name left in the air, no residue.

I whisper your name a second time and, again, it is taken and absorbed. I lie still, listening. It is like deep water, this silence. I am on my back, my head is square on the pillow, my arms and hands are exposed to the air and resting by my sides, and my eyes are open to the empty darkness all around. I lift my fingers. I wonder if I could dip my fingers into this silence. I lift both my hands so that they are suspended above the bed. I feel sure that if I could dip my fingers into this silence, it would feel like cool water. Cool water from a dark and bottomless well.

JASPER

There was something about the acoustics on Tremore Crescent. More than a year since we moved out and here I am, thinking about acoustics. The way the valley dipped at the reserve like a skate park, houses propped on the edges. Dotted through the reserve were saplings, held by forged steel cages so that in winter, when they lost their leaves, they were like skeletons behind bars. Sounds would ricochet through that dip and around those bars and into all those open-plan living areas, bedrooms, bathrooms. All those fucking bathrooms. It wasn't just the barking dogs. There were lawnmowers, blower vacs and whipper snippers, the odd kid throwing a tantrum, adult yelling, stereo turned up too loud.

What I've been wondering is this: were the barking dogs even the real problem? Or was it something else, something you wouldn't think of – like, acoustics? Can you blame a problem on acoustics like people blame alcohol or insanity? Or a malfunctioning traffic light?

This is what I think about, lying alone at night, Ella and Braydon asleep in the new bunk next to me.

I still sometimes double-check locks; do double-takes in the main street. And I ask myself: should I be worried? Should I be scared?

We lived in Tremore Crescent for eleven months. I pick over those months like that old fella on the bike picks over everyone's rubbish. I think about them when I'm lining up at the checkout or when I'm feeding one of the old people and waiting for them to swallow.

~

No one thought about acoustics at the very beginning, when they built those houses. There was no thinking when those houses were built. Some things, unbelievable. Like the way the laundry tap and basin were just out of reach of where any washing machine – not just our old Westinghouse – could possibly have fit. We had to use hoses to connect it up. They always got kinks and holes in them, and the whole room would flood. A bit of a problem when you consider our dodgy clothes dryer was just sitting on the floor.

Other things were less obvious: the way the house was sited on the block meant the view was just missed; had the kitchen window been five centimetres to the left, I could have seen that lovely tree next door when I was washing the dishes, instead of the garage wall. It was always cold in winter and hot in summer, no matter how much we turned the reverse-cycle up or down. The house was more like the brochure of a house, or the idea of a house.

Everybody's yards have some kind of slope in Tremore Crescent, either at the front or back of the house. Pretty much all kit homes but some flash ones too. Big, showy gardens – moss rocks, retaining walls, roses. McMansions. I've only come across that word this week. A McMansion is all impressive to look at but you could knock it over with a feather. I know because we watched one being built.

Tremore Crescent bends like a horseshoe, both ends meeting at Beecroft Way, which winds around the estate like a vine, sending off crescents, ways, closes and courts with most of them ending in a cul-de-sac. I was disappointed the street names weren't themed and, even now, I occasionally find myself reciting the names in my head, sitting in a doctor's office or outside Braydon's classroom, trying to find a link between them. I'm pretty sure there isn't one.

We used to go for walks after tea. We'd walk to Beecroft Way and follow it until we came to Cherrybrook Close, chosen on our first walk because we liked the name.

We'd admire everyone else's gardens and then take Pedrick Way, and then Huon Close, where we'd stop for a bit to watch progress on the McMansion before walking back to Tremore. It took no more than two months. The McMansion was up so fast you could've blinked and missed some crucial part – framing, blue board, windows, final lick of that gold-yellow paint they all like to use. You could take a tour of an old English history book walking those streets, all the different styles were there – Tudor, Victorian, Georgian – you name it. My favourite was the Australian colonial style on Cherrybrook Close, with the wide verandahs. They've got big old cane chairs and those trees with the tiny little storybook oranges in terracotta pots, one on either side of the front door. The first time me and the kids saw that house we decided we'd get one of those pots with one of those trees. We would say it whenever we walked past. 'We're getting one of those, aren't we, Mum?' Braydon would say. Or Ella would point and say, 'There!'

We never got one. And they're called cumquats. They're evergreen and you can eat the fruit – apparently they make good jam. I saw one the other day at the nursery on the intersection between Hutchinson Street and McLaren Street. It was in a wooden half wine barrel against the back gate. I read the bit about the jam on a tag wired on the trunk.

You might have thought we were renters in Gladeview Park estate – Nathan and the kids and me – and if you saw me now, you'd be more certain of it. We weren't.

Out of nowhere – it was late spring and we were in the middle of a weird heatwave, high thirties, low forties for five days running – a formal letter arrived, addressed to Nathan Hearle. We were scratchy, cooped up in the Haydn Street rental, no air conditioner there or street trees for shade. The letter gave us a bit of a distraction while we waited for Nathan to get home and open it. Braydon was six then, home from school with chicken pox. Not really sick, just a few scaly spots. He was sure that Nathan had got a speeding ticket. That was before he started calling him 'Dad'. Ella was nearly three and she thought Daddy had won the lotto. She was close. He'd inherited seventy grand. A fortune.

An aunt he barely knew he had – his dad's youngest sister. Patricia. She lived in Townsville. Never married or had a family of her own and decided to give all the nephews an equal share of her money. Tracey, Nathan's sister, wasn't left any. No one had seen her for several years, so I'm guessing she never found out about it.

I never met Tracey. Only saw her picture the day we went to Nathan's dad's house in Kingscote. I was just pregnant with Ella and I will always remember it because of that metallic saliva in my mouth, that foul spinning in my head like I'd spent days on a show ride, the colour of my spew as it traced down the grilled floor of the ferry – red, from all the lolly snakes I'd been eating.

Their mum died in her mid-forties – lung cancer, though they said she'd never smoked a cigarette – and you'd think, being pregnant, that I would have found this sad, being in Nathan's family home, but no. I felt too sick to think or feel anything.

In the picture, Tracey was standing next to her. They both had black hair, but Tracey's was dyed an even darker black, blue-black. You could see the tips of a large-looking tattoo poking up through her tank top. Their mum was thin, a wrap around her head. Tracey looked like she'd left her body in the photo and gone somewhere else. Not a happy photo, but for some reason it was the one Rodney had chosen to put in a frame. Someone'd glued little shells all round the edges. I'm not big on that crafty stuff.

Nathan had hovered behind me when I looked at that picture. I could feel his muscles tightening. He was looking at the picture over my shoulder and then turning his head to study my expression and then back to the picture. I think he was hoping I might remember his mum. I didn't recognise her at all. How could I? I'd only lived on the island for eighteen months, when we were hiding from my dad.

The truth was, Nathan and I had practically got together on the basis that we'd both lived in Kingscote. And that we had the same taste in potato chips. Two great coincidences. So why not have a child right away and move in together?

I was having a drink at Grays Inn to farewell one of the nurses. Braydon was staying the night at Mum's down in the city. I was letting my hair down. It'd been a while and I was out of practice – tipsy after two glasses. I made my way to the front bar, thinking I'd get a packet of chips, something to line my stomach before I drank anything else. It was packed. The guys in the front bar sounded like engines revving. You could have shouted anything and no one would have heard. I pushed my way through and pointed to the chips on a metal rack bolted to the back wall, handed over five dollars.

I felt a nudge in my waist; it wasn't part of the general pushing and shoving. I felt a shiver go through me, and then this voice right up close to my ear, this deep, gentle voice like a movie star's. 'Madam, I think you just got the last packet of sour cream and chives.'

I didn't move for a bit, his warm breath on my neck. I had the spins. I turned slowly and our faces were so close, almost touching. He smiled: one tooth was slightly brown, but strangely, even that was attractive. He leant into my neck again.

'My favourite too,' he said.

He was buff. Black jeans and a dark grey shirt, tucked in. Arms sinewy and strong. I liked the tattoos. He looked tough, but also neat. I liked that. I'd never met anyone like that.

We left the front bar and went out onto the street, and after a bit of chitchat we discovered we'd both gone to Kingscote area school. I was only two years older than Nathan but as much as we tried, we couldn't remember each other. I couldn't remember Tracey either, but then she was four years older than me. It didn't matter. I'd never met anyone else whose favourite chips were sour cream and chives. That, and the shiver, and fucking Kingscote.

We were freaked out by all these coincidences. Like it was magic, or something. We never said, 'It was meant to be,' but that's how we felt. It was more of a thing we tried on, like an expensive coat neither of us would normally buy. I remember it was a full moon, too.

~

After the letter and eventually the money, things moved quickly, things I didn't even know were in the pipeline. Apparently Nathan had had this idea for a while. He wanted to be the kind of man who lived in one of those houses in one of those streets with the big entrance pillars that you see council workers weeding around and scrubbing the graffiti off one day after it gets sprayed.

Number Twelve Tremore Crescent had been on the market for months. He'd been watching it, apparently. He said it had potential, that it hadn't yet reached its full value and that's why it was a good buy. He could have said that it was the worst house in the best street, like Gary, the real estate agent said to us – *large family home in desirable blue ribbon location* were the exact words printed on the sign – but he didn't, because he didn't *want* to live in the worst house.

He couldn't really afford it, the repayments, but he bought it anyway with his $70,000 deposit and got himself a whopping mortgage. I say 'he' because my name wasn't on the title. Even though I made most of the repayments over that twelve-month period. I'd just started at the local nursing home as an aide and I mostly did the night shift, sleeping – trying to sleep – during the day.

We first heard the dogs on Friday 14 January. The day we were meant to move in. Settlement was on Thursday, and Gary met us at the house with the keys and the gift basket.

'Congratulations, guys!' Gary said, but he wasn't really looking at us when he said it. He had two sets of keys in one hand and the basket in the other, and he was fumbling with the front door lock, much more awkwardly and dramatically than I thought was really necessary. It would have been easier if he'd put the basket down or handed it to us. I guess he wanted to make a song and dance about it once we were inside the house.

Looking back, there must have been at least one dog barking then, because I know now that the dog at Number Seven would have been able to see this little commotion going on at our front door. But I don't remember this. I don't remember any barking when we went to the open inspections either, which is a mystery.

Gary's movements were quick and jerky, his pinstripe suit jacket flapping about. We were all slow and dreamy, and we were the ones who really should have been excited. Nathan was very quiet but he also seemed agitated. I kept watching him from the corner of my eye. Gary was flashing him quick looks too. Was Nathan disappointed? Was it not what he expected? Did the house seem different from when we'd been to the opens? Was he just overwhelmed by how much debt he was in? I don't know.

Within seconds of Gary's Mazda pulling out of the driveway, before we'd even had a chance to walk around Nathan's new house or catch our breath, Braydon came running down the passage, a strange twisted look on his face, chocolate around his mouth. Ella was behind him, not running, looking very wrong. I made a weird sound that I couldn't describe or repeat. Like a scream but not like the ones on TV; mine was low and ugly. Then I was screeching.

'Jesus! Fucking Jesus! What's wrong with her? What happened? What happened?'

I was digging around in my handbag for my phone. I was going to call an ambulance.

Nathan pushed past me and Braydon and grabbed Ella. He didn't make any sound at all.

Ella's face was almost unrecognisable; her eyes were puffy slits and her whole head was bright pink with white welts around her mouth and cheeks. And her lips were swollen. She opened them to say, 'Daddy,' her voice gravelly like an old smoker's.

'In the car! Get in the car!' Nathan's voice was deep and angry. I closed my bag, wrapped my arm around Braydon's head and pulled him outside. I don't think we even locked the house behind us. Nathan carried Ella and put her on my lap in the front seat. I sat there clutching her and crying. Nathan drove straight to the hospital in town and into the side lane for ambulances. He didn't look at me or Ella once, not once. 'Fierce' is the only word I can think of. It was like he'd been waiting for the whole thing to happen and he'd been saving his energy for that moment. He was like the hero in an action movie and I was some pathetic extra they got to sob in the background. None of it seemed real. Even at the hospital, he was practically giving orders to the nurses. But thank God, they knew what to do. Adrenaline and antihistamine, the stuff that's now in my handbag and at Ella's preschool. She was looking normal again within an hour but they wanted to watch her, so she and I spent the night in hospital. I lay awake, going over what happened and thinking about Nathan. Ella looks exactly like him. She especially did then, because she hadn't grown much hair and he shaves his off. Same heart-shaped face, dimpled chin, bright blue eyes, although Nathan's two front teeth cross each other slightly and that one on the left is nearly black. Ella has perfect tiny white teeth and I can't imagine her having anything different. Her skin is pink and soft. Nathan is tanned, with heavy black tattoos across his shoulders, down his arms and on each knuckle – symbols, mostly, but he was always vague about them.

Nathan and Braydon stayed on the lounge-room floor of my friend Deb's that night. I didn't love the plan, but all our stuff was either in the truck we borrowed or sitting on the front driveway of our rental in Haydn Street, waiting to be picked up in the second round.

So it wasn't until the Friday that we actually spent our first night in Tremore Crescent. A hot, still night. I remember the sounds of grasshoppers and frogs, like tapping on a hollow log. Peaceful, I thought, like a nature CD. We turned the air conditioner down to 18 degrees and sat in the lounge watching telly, flicking around the channels without really getting into anything, boxes all over the floor, some opened, some not. We didn't know then how bloody expensive it was to run that Panasonic air conditioner. You can't believe those fucking star rating stickers. That's one thing I've learnt.

I found the rest of the gift basket in our walk-in robe. There were chocolate bullets and raspberry licorice, a bottle of champagne, crackers, pretzels and, of course, the last of the salted peanuts. Nathan scooped it up with one hand and put the whole thing in the wheelie bin outside. I could've used the basket for something. And I wouldn't've minded the champagne. I didn't say anything. I suppose he was just thinking of Ella. We were told we had to be careful of cross contamination now and we still had to get tests done to see if she was allergic to any other nuts. I don't see how peanut dust could've got *into* an unopened champagne bottle.

So the dogs started after tea. We'd had Macca's and we were left with that not-so-great feeling after you've eaten a Big Mac and fries. I say the dogs started after tea but only because Nathan told me a couple of hours later. I hadn't heard them. I had tuned out without even registering the sound. I can do that. Nathan can't.

It was about a quarter to ten. The kids had gone to sleep on the floor, and I was making the beds up with sheets, too hot for doonas. Nathan was nowhere. I checked all the rooms and then I spotted him through the laundry sliding door. He was pacing up and down on the back verandah, his arms held out from his body. His head was stooped, his eyebrows crunched into one dark line. He looked wild. When I tapped on the glass his head shot up so fast he must've cricked his neck.

I pulled open the door. 'Hun, what's wrong?' I asked. I'd known him for more than three years. More than three years, the longest I'd been with anyone. I'd never seen him look like that.

'Those bloody dogs.' He said it through his teeth.

I tuned in and, yep, there were a number of dogs barking. Maybe three or four, you could hear the variations. One deep, more like a walrus than a dog, a couple of rhythmic ones, like broken records, maybe one closer to us than the others, some high-pitched, yappy barks. Sounded like they were coming from across the reserve and over the road. Overall, yeah, it was annoying when you put it all together, when you focused on it and started to expect it in the nerve endings of your brain. Which is what Nathan was doing.

'It's heaps worse out here,' I told him. 'Come inside. You can hardly hear them inside.' I told him he had to come in because I needed help carrying the kids to bed.

He squinted like he was looking at me through smoke. It crossed my mind to offer him one – I still kept a stash – but Nathan didn't smoke, never had. I gave up when I met him because he said it repulsed him to see a woman smoking.

I'm making up for it now, though – smoking more than I ever did before.

When he finally came inside, I noticed his bottom lip pulled up tight under his front teeth. And his shoulders were squared and seemed bigger. When I locked the laundry door behind him, I stood for a minute, just listening. The barking was still there, but faded. I practised tuning in and tuning out. It wasn't that bloody hard.

Ella was heavy in my arms, really asleep. I couldn't believe it was less than twenty-four hours ago that she'd been in hospital. No wonder we were tired. Her skin was cool against mine, her baby hair in damp curls around her face. I loved her so much right then, it sort of upset me. You can love someone so much that it actually hurts. I laid her on the bed and leant into her face. She'd eaten fast food and hadn't brushed her teeth, but her breath was sweet still.

Nathan was ripping masking tape off another box. He was still shitty when I came back into the lounge.

'Hey, it's not that bad,' I said. 'Is it?'

He rolled the tape between his hands until it made a ball and threw it across the kitchen bench onto the floor.

'Well, it's not exactly good, is it? If they're gonna carry on like that, we're never gonna get any peace at all, are we? *Serene and fun-filled living*, my arse.'

This was written on the sign at the entrance to the estate. It's still there. A red-brick wall on either side of the road curves inwards like the welcoming gesture of two outstretched arms, a gold plaque with black writing on each: *Gladeview Park* on one, *Serene and Fun-Filled Living* on the other.

It's asking for trouble, putting that on a sign. Words on a plaque are like a promise. Maybe that was the problem: the barking dogs were like a broken promise.

I went into the kitchen and closed the sliding window.

Climbing up the glass was a tiny frog. First one I'd ever seen.

'Nath, check this out!' I wished the kids were still awake. I'd only ever heard frogs before. It was about two centimetres long, a dark charcoal colour. Unless you saw it move like I just had, you could have easily thought it was a bit of leaf or dirt stuck to the glass.

Nathan came up behind me, leant into the window and whistled through his teeth. 'Well, there you go,' he said, and he pulled my head back slightly and kissed my hair. 'Whatever makes you happy, babe.' He went back to the boxes shaking his head and smiling.

We saw lots of frogs for a couple of months, then it got cold again and they disappeared.

Me and the kids've only got a tiny backyard now, no garden, no frogs. I can walk it from front to back and side to side with five steps each way. It's just flattened dry grass with dirt patches, a thin line of cement around the unit like a skirt that's too short. Jacquie at work reckons that frogs mean the environment is clean, because frogs can't survive with any kind of pollution. I used to think of that when I saw Braydon and Ella in the garden at Tremore Crescent. Like if there were frogs, I was a good mum. The frogs were an omen that my kids were safe.

It wasn't really a garden at Number Twelve, more a yard. Not like the neighbour's with their big trees and paths and rose bushes and bulbs in the spring. All those jonquils and daffodils and the tulips – tulips are the expensive ones. Our yard was just as big, around half an acre, but ours was bare except for one straggly tree in the middle. I don't think anyone actually planted it. It must've just blown in one day.

~

Well, it wasn't long before the trampoline arrived. Nathan bought it on eBay. It was one of those large, round trampolines with the safety netting. The netting never arrived, but the kids loved it, especially Braydon. He said that when he jumped he could see the rooftops and into the yards of everyone else's houses on the street.

Three weeks later, the Permapine cubbyhouse was delivered. I don't know where it came from – it just turned up on the back of a truck. Nathan got them to drive across the reserve so they could lower it over our back fence. He was like the foreman, lifting his arm high in the air and giving instructions to the driver. He looked around a lot, as though he was expecting someone else to show up. I'd just got back from the nursing home and had that bleary-eyed, heavy feeling you get after a long, hard shift. Edna Oates had died, and it's going to sound mean but deaths just involve a lot more work, a lot of lifting and cleaning, even for the aides like me who don't have to do the paperwork.

Nathan bought a lot of things in those first few months at Tremore Crescent. I didn't know how he was paying for it all, but we weren't so worried about money at first, 'cause we were on the honeymoon interest rate. Maybe he'd kept a little of the inheritance aside, not put all of it into the house deposit – I didn't know.

I asked him, when the pool came from Kmart. We had to put it up on the back verandah because the backyard had too much slope on it.

'We'll excavate that later,' Nathan said.

'How much was it, Nath?'

He was holding the hose, attached to the tap on the back of the house, slowly filling the pool with water.

'Cost enough, babe. It cost enough.' He smiled at me and winked.

What happened to the pool, or the cubby, or the trampoline? I don't even know. They were like three weird lonely questions in our backyard. Why, why and why. Nathan probably thought of them as statements. They were statements about the kind of father he was, the kind of man. He was a man who lived in Gladeview Park estate, whose children had a pool, a trampoline and a cubby.

If you can't afford something, then you don't have it. That's how I was raised. I'm not saying it was fun, but me and Mum never had debt. I'll give her that.

~

'It's always the way, Kelly,' Mum said to me when I arrived late at night, the kids asleep on the back seat of the Corolla, all our clothes stuffed in the boot. She was wearing her old pink dressing-gown, but she was wide awake, like she'd been expecting me, like she'd been expecting me for the last three and a half years. 'They're all arseholes, love ...'

'Yep,' I cut her off. 'Thanks. Thanks, Mum. I get it.' I was exhausted by then, but also strangely calm. I was like one of the doctors who swing by the nursing home on a Saturday night to sign the death certificate, all cool and efficient, like it's nothing.

Sometimes you see the wives through the window, waiting in the car in their lipstick and pearls.

I didn't sleep until after midnight, which means – I calculated this only today – I hadn't slept for over thirty-six hours on that day.

We drove to my friend Deb's first. I told her that Nathan and I had had a fight, and she looked at me sideways and squinted. Did she smile? Maybe she did. She had another friend over, Tara, and they were drinking Vodka Cruisers, laughing about having to walk to the school for pick-up. I just wanted some kind of quiet.

We only stayed with Mum for two weeks; I couldn't stand it. I wanted to be back where we'd made a home, up in the Barker. I didn't want to start all over again, someplace new. I would have missed this place if we'd stayed down in the city, not being near trees and farms and all the big gardens. I rang the nursing home, said I'd caught scarlet fever from Ella, which miraculously bought me three weeks off, without more questions, and a job to go back to.

I'm beating round the bush with this, I know. 'Cut to the chase, Kel,' Nathan used to say. I prefer to circle, move in to the hard part slowly, go over and over, until I get it.

~

Deb used to go on and on about how lucky I was to have a guy like Nathan.

'Think about it, Kelly,' she'd say, 'Braydon's not even his, but he treats both of them like they are. Braydon doesn't even look like him. He's the best dad. You are one lucky lady.'

She was right about Braydon not looking like Nathan. He's slight, like me, with my hazel eyes and sandy-coloured hair, thick too. Braydon's sticks up everywhere. Skin that burns easily. He doesn't look anything like his real dad. He was part Maori – you wouldn't have known it, though. We looked like one of those families where one kid looks like the mum and the other kid looks like the dad – mini-me's – but in those perfect families, where everyone has nice clothes and the kids play musical instruments, the girl always looks like the mum. We had it arse-up. I'll always see Nathan when I look at Ella.

Deb, I haven't seen Deb for over a year now.

The swimming pool delivery was around the time that Nathan joined the Mount Barker Summit Club. Another mystery in itself. He started spending his days planning sausage sizzles for the Mitre 10 carpark on the weekend: drawing up rosters, ordering huge amounts of cheap meat, driving to the Council chambers to negotiate permissions. Or he'd be laying bricks for new public seating in the wetlands or organising a backyard blitz for some sad and sorry lady in town. It was like a job, except that he didn't get paid. He used to wear the orange polo top on weekdays. On the top right-hand side of his chest was a brown- and green-striped triangle, with *Summit* written in the middle. The three sides of the triangle represent the ideals of service, citizenship and friendship, and the actual word 'Summit' isn't just the highest point of Mount Barker, but also represents ambition and personal success. That's what Nathan told me.

When I explained the triangle to Deb, she sat on my

kitchen bar stool shaking her head and said, 'God.'

Nathan started talking about inviting his Summit friends around for a barbecue.

'We can't afford to have that many people over for a barbecue,' I told him.

'It's all good,' Nathan said. 'You just make it BYO, that's what they do.'

We never had the BYO barbecue.

The barking seemed to be getting worse.

From the moment we drove our Corolla into the carport, one dog in particular would start barking. When the postie came to our letterbox, or one of us stepped outside and, especially, if anyone or anything new came to our house, like when the truck delivered the cubby, this one dog would bark and bark, a mid-range yap, over and over, literally, some days it went for hours. On the worst, this dog would set off all the other dogs whose owners must've been at work. And then you'd get the whole carry-on. Probably me and Nathan were the only ones at home during the day in that whole place.

Even still, I could tune it out. Dogs bark, that's what they do, you just get on with it. Oddly enough, it was the days when I had been on nights and was trying to sleep that Nathan found it hardest. He said it was 'outrageous' because people who did shift work needed to sleep during the day. He would get so angry, pacing up and down the hallway, thumping a wall, sighing dramatically, that he was the only reason I couldn't get any sleep. I only wanted the dog to stop so Nathan would stop.

One late morning in June, after I had spent the last couple of hours in bed, my eyes shut tight, listening to Nathan swearing and carrying on, I gave up and got up. Nathan was leaning over the laminex kitchen bench, his arms stretched out wide, his head low, like he was swimming butterfly stroke. I put my hand on the back of his shoulder. He swung around so fast, my hand went flying back and hit the wall cupboard behind me.

'Right!' he snapped. 'That's it! That's the final straw! This is outrageous!' He grabbed the car keys from the kitchen bench where I'd left them two hours before and marched out the front door.

I heard the Corolla reverse, sharp brake and screech off.

He didn't go far. I stood at the laundry window watching him as he drove slowly up and down Beecroft Way. His window was down – it looked as though half his body was leaning out – and I'm guessing he was trying to see behind people's backyard fences. Then he got out of the car and disappeared. He'd started knocking on doors. It didn't occur to him to look on our street. He was sure the barking was coming from the other side of the reserve. When he came back an hour later, he was furious, his nose flaring and his shoulders pulled back so hard I could see the blades meeting through his jacket. He'd found a German shepherd, a kelpie and a pair of little yappy dogs. (Pomeranians, I think. They're still there.)

Nathan told me the woman from Number Twenty-Four was 'a total bitch'. He shook his fingers out like they were cramping and rolled his neck around. 'I just told her there was a problem with dogs barking and I was trying to get to the bottom of it, and she told me to piss off. Closed the door in my face.'

I looked down at his knuckles. 'You know, Nath, if someone didn't know you, hun, you could come across as a bit scary.'

'What?'

He seemed hurt. He held up his knuckles and inspected them, as if he was discovering his tattoos for the first time.

'These aren't scary,' he said. 'They're peaceful symbols.'

I felt sorry for him.

~

Money was getting tighter, my night shift had been cut back to three or four a week, there didn't seem to be any roof plumbing work around for Nathan anymore – now that all the smaller estates had mostly gone up in town, only farmland left now. We were getting Family Tax Benefit part A and B, but barely scraping together the mortgage, even when we went to interest only. Then we got our second electricity bill. I sometimes wondered what those Summit people thought Nathan did for a job. I would have, if I was one of them. How many people could do volunteer work on weekdays? Besides retirees? I used to go for walks in the wetlands and look at people with their dogs, and I'd think, How do they keep it all together? Pay their mortgages? Keep it all going? Is it this hard for everyone else? But I knew it wasn't. Those people walking their dogs looked like they had the secret to life or something. I don't go to the wetlands so much anymore.

Ella's child care was the logical thing to cut – I was mostly home during the day (even if I was trying to sleep), and so was Nathan.

The day after we made that decision, a second-hand bright red tandem bike arrived at our house, multicoloured streamers coming out of each of the handlebars.

'My God!' Deb said when she first saw them riding back up Tremore Crescent, flash new helmets and Ella's big grin, holding onto her own set of handlebars behind her dad, her feet perched up on little bars that stuck out on the side. 'You can't buy them like him, Kel,' she said, 'he's a keeper, an absolute keeper.' She put her coffee mug down on the kitchen bench and her eyes widened in a sort of 'I told you so' way.

Even my mum shook her head in disbelief when she came up and saw them riding that bike down our street. 'I wouldn't've said it, Kel, with those tattoos and that look in the eye, but I think you might've hit the jackpot this time, love.' And then she pulled at my sleeve and patted my arm, which made me nervous.

The bike gave me the idea that maybe Nathan and Ella could deliver catalogues or newspapers or something. I'd seen an ad in the local paper: *Keep Fit and Earn Money. Earn $100–$200 per week. 8–10 hours delivering and collecting catalogues. No outlay.* I didn't think the money was that bad. It was definitely something, and we could have used anything.

Nathan was parking the bike in the garage when I mentioned it, and he swung around. 'I will never be so desperate that I have to deliver the freakin' newspaper. Or junk mail! Or bloody Avon! Are you serious? That's a job for kids, Kelly ... kids!'

And yet there he was, riding around like a what? Like a bloody kid, that's what. Who rides a tandem bike around the streets with coloured tassels hanging out of the handlebars?

We were desperate. It wasn't just the money, either. A week

after Nathan went looking for the dog, our letterbox went missing. A crappy metal one on a stick, so it was an easy target; not like the bricked-in letterboxes on the rest of the street.

Nathan started going for walks at night, keeping his eye on Number Twenty-Four Beecroft Way. The woman had teenage sons – cars with P-plates came and went. Nathan decided that one of them had stolen our letterbox. I told him that he might be right but maybe not. It might have just been kids mucking around, having fun.

Soon he was walking every night, stalking slowly around the streets surrounding our house. Sometimes, from the laundry door, I could see him across the reserve when he passed under a streetlight. Every now and then he'd stop, turn quickly, stop again, moving like a bird. He was still trying to work out the major source of the barking.

He found it the following week.

He and Ella had gone for a walk during the day while I tried to get some rest. Before I'd had any chance to even fall asleep, the front door opened and slammed shut, and I heard the sliding door from the lounge being pushed open. I came out to see what was going on and saw Nathan in the backyard, Ella trailing after him, a bewildered look on her face. Nathan ran down the bank and back up again. He leapt onto the trampoline and started jumping. Then he got off the trampoline and, using the side fence as leverage, climbed onto the cubby roof. He was dodging this way and that and straining his neck in the direction of the house at the top of our street. Number Seven. Finally, he jumped down, scooped Ella up into a piggyback and bounded to the back door.

'It's a fluffball mongrel!' He pointed toward Number Seven. He was puffing hard, grinning like a madman.

Ella was grinning too and watching me closely. Nathan cupped his ear with his hand, she tightened her grip around his neck, and then he held his palm up to the sky. 'Do you get it?'

I was so tired I couldn't think straight.

'That barking,' he said forcefully, 'is coming from there!' He pushed his chin up. 'The mongrel is there!'

The 'mongrel' was actually one of those designer dogs, honey coloured. I put designer dogs into Google Images at work and I reckon it was a groodle. A groodle is a cross between a golden retriever and a poodle. He was called Jasper. I know that now, but I didn't know it then.

I drove past Jasper's house the other day. I don't know why I do this, I truly don't, but sometimes I drive up Beecroft Way, take a loop around Tremore Crescent and then back into Beecroft and out again.

Number Seven has one of those gardens that uses mostly natives and has a *Rain Water in Use* sign. I want to say: I don't care what water you use. *Relax, go your hardest.* Back then, you couldn't see any dirt; it was all green and smoky greys, yellow greens, rusted reds, even black. Lots of different shapes and angles. There were native grasses that some people might think of as weeds, but you knew that the owners of Number Seven wouldn't. And then, in spring, through all that hardy dark ground cover and the leafy curls with little purple flowers, daffodils poked up randomly around the whole front garden.

Now the grevilleas have grown so bushy, it's hard to see the front door. The Subaru's gone, and there's a Pajero. I don't know whether this means the owners sold or whether they bought a new car. I wonder whether people who grow natives and put in rainwater tanks would buy a brand-new four-wheel drive. Isn't that a contradiction? Just another one of life's little mysteries. I sometimes feel as though I'm surrounded with all these little mysteries that have to be solved, even ones that I've created myself. Just a whole lot of dumb little mysteries. They occur to me throughout the day, but also they are in my dreams. In my dreams I have to search for useless lost objects and analyse things for clues. I think so hard it feels like I'm awake. And then the objects morph into Braydon or Ella and suddenly it's my kids who are lost and I'm like the detective in charge on some cop show, but no one else is there to help and none of the clues make any sense. On and on it goes. I wake up feeling like shit.

Does the Pajero mean the owners sold and moved? Who knows.

Nathan used to say I should have been a copper the way I get so involved when I'm reading the paper or watching the news on telly.

'You're just right into it all, aren't you, Kel?' he'd say. 'You've got one big imagination,' and he'd rub my shoulder or ruffle my hair, his hand trailing down my back, drawing little circles. I used to love it when he did stuff like that. Everything felt good then. Sometimes it was hard to imagine I'd ever be on my own again. I'm not saying I don't miss him. I'm not saying I don't miss him at night, when the kids are asleep.

~

Nathan didn't care much about the mystery of the missing letterbox after that. We picked up another one from a cheap online shop that delivered free. Nathan stopped stalking the streets and put all his energy into Jasper.

First thing he did was ring the Council. They said he should approach the owners and if they didn't stop the barking, he could record and document it, put together a grievance case against them. They couldn't have given Nathan worse advice. Twice he went to Number Seven to speak to the owners but both times nobody was home, so he skipped this step and started recording the barking onto an old voice recorder he picked up from Cash Converters.

It became part of Ella's routine, like story-time or fruit snack might have been at child care. Nathan would drive Braydon to school, then he would put the recorder in a backpack and he and Ella would ride around the block on the tandem bike, stopping in front of Number Seven, where they'd record the dog going ballistic for fifteen minutes (because they were standing in front of it!) and then they'd come home. Ella would say, 'I get the book, Dadda,' and she'd trot into the bedroom and retrieve the little exercise book that Nathan kept next to his side of the bed and take it into the dining room where he'd document the barking. Then she'd draw squiggles next to it on the opposite page. Finally, she'd replace the book in the bedroom. I'd be lying in the bed pretending to be asleep – wondering, among other things, why Nathan insisted on keeping the book in the bedroom where I was trying to sleep. Then they'd repeat the whole thing in the afternoon while Braydon was watching television or doing his spelling matrix.

For a while, weirdly, it seemed to calm things down. Nathan felt he was 'doing something about the barking', even though, in reality, I'd say he was making it worse. I knew how long they stood in that driveway because the barking was so loud, even I couldn't tune it out.

I saw the owners once. I was going for a walk on a Saturday early that spring. I hadn't really given the seasons much thought until the year we lived in Gladeview Park estate. I'd never really seen what happens in gardens before. I was learning the names of flowers and plants. Braydon and I would test each other and occasionally we would stop off at the nursery on the way home from school to read the labels. Everyone's jonquils were up and starting to wilt and the daffodils were starting to open.

They were weeding out the front, all three of them, even the boy. He only looked about Braydon's age, maybe a little older. You could tell he was an only child, that he'd never had to fight anyone for anything. Thin with dark straight hair that flopped around his face. The mum wore a floppy sunhat. The man looked like a big version of the boy, and smart – a teacher, probably.

I liked the way they were all working together in the garden. Even the dog sat watching from their back gate. He started barking but stopped when the boy went over and leant into the wire. The woman looked up from beneath the brim of her hat and smiled at me. 'Hi,' she said, and it was so friendly and happy that I smiled back, but I couldn't get a sound to come out of my mouth. I was trying to imagine a voice inside me that might match hers and I couldn't find one. She went back to her work, so I kept walking back to our place.

Why didn't I say anything? Why didn't I tell Nathan they were home? I can't explain it, even now. There was just something I didn't want to mess with. I didn't want us to be in that picture – our money stress or any of our problems. I didn't want Nathan to be part of that picture. Looking back now, I wonder what might have happened differently if I'd said something. Maybe I knew it wouldn't have changed anything.

~

One month later. Tuesday. Braydon was at school. Ella was playing in the cubby with a handful of dolls and some old saucepans we'd bought from the Salvos. I'd been home from night shift for a couple of hours, had put a quick load of washing through.

To this day, the whir of the washing machine going through a cycle, the swish of the water, the rolling of the metal drum, can make me feel on edge. I haven't told anybody this, but for a while I used a laundromat just so the sound of a washing machine wouldn't be in my house.

I was sitting down at the kitchen bench having a cup of coffee with Nathan. I was drinking chamomile tea but if I'd known I wasn't going to be getting any sleep that day, I might have had a Nescafé too. We heard that strained hum of the postie's scooter making the turn from Beecroft Way into Tremore Crescent. Nathan jumped off his stool and headed out the front door. I assumed he was going to collect our mail. We only ever got bills.

The door clicked closed. The barking started. A minute or so passed, and then Nathan returned and slid an opened letter onto the bench. I saw the blue and yellow logo of the Adelaide bank.

I leant back on my stool to spot Ella through the window. She was happily lining up her dolls on the balcony of the cubbyhouse, pointing a finger at them, one by one, her small lips moving around words.

The postie had obviously stopped at Number Seven by now, because the barking was crazy. Methodical. Nathan rubbed his shaved head hard with his knuckles. He closed his eyes and rocked back on his heels, opened them again and pushed the letter closer to me. I suddenly felt very tired, the kind of tired where you wonder if you can keep your eyes open at all, when your eyelids ache with their own weight. I scanned the letter. One of their consultants had been trying to call us but our phone had been disconnected.

I had no idea our phone had been disconnected. I must've only been using my mobile. Did Nathan know about the phone? The letter said that the bank hadn't been able to inform us that our mortgage repayments were now in arrears by over two months.

'Why's our mortgage in arrears?' I asked him.

Money was tight, but I knew I'd been making enough, with the Centrelink payments, to just manage the mortgage, as long as we were careful with everything else. But this was bad. If we were behind, there was no way I could fix it.

The dog was still barking. It wasn't really bothering me, I was focusing on the letter, but I couldn't tune it out completely like I normally could. Nathan was rubbing his head again. And he was biting at his lips, rolling them around with his teeth.

He slammed his hand on the bench. I jumped a little on my stool, leant back again to check on Ella: she was filling a saucepan with dirt at the side of the cubby.

I glared at him.

Something snapped inside my head, something brittle. Everything, all of it, just seemed so stupid. So stupid and unnecessary. I started yelling at him, trying to smother the volume through my teeth. 'Nathan, settle down! We'll sort it out. You'll have to go to the bank and talk to them about it. You'll have to make a plan. And you're going to have to take that job. You know you are.'

The last bit was the wrong thing to say.

Nathan had been offered work at the abattoir in Lobethal. A mate, Dan, who used to get him the roof plumbing work, had been there for about three months and had lined up a sure thing for Nathan. The pay was actually good, and the hours we could have worked around. He'd knocked it back. He'd said that he didn't believe in cutting up animals. He'd said that he wasn't going to stand around with a bunch of Asians who couldn't have a yarn at lunchtime because they couldn't speak bloody English. He'd said he was too good for it.

We'd already had an argument about it, which is why I shouldn't have said what I said next. I was doing calculations in my head. I knew my hourly rate, I knew how many hours I'd worked in the last month, I knew how much money should have been in that account. I was watching him, numbers and questions tumbling around. Nathan kept chewing on his lips and his breath was coming out of his nose so loud and hard he sounded like a tetchy horse. The dog barked over the top of it all.

And then I said it – no, I yelled it. 'Do you know what, Nathan? You're not too good for it! You are so-not-too-fucking-good for it!'

I wasn't pointing my finger into his chest, but I might as well have been. And if I wasn't so angry, I might have felt like crying.

His nostrils flared. He stared at me so hard and his eyes were so fierce that, for the first time, I felt scared. Without moving his eyes, he reached across the bench to the wooden Wiltshire knife block and pulled out our largest knife.

My heart started thumping. It was too late to take back what I'd said.

He stood motionless, his eyes locked on mine, the knife held in front of both our faces.

He lowered the knife and walked out the front door. I didn't move for another moment. A sob came up in my chest but didn't make it out of my mouth.

I checked for Ella. She was back on the balcony, sitting against the wall with one of the dolls in her lap, stroking its hair.

The rest of my memory about that morning isn't a line of events, of what happened next and then what happened after that. I only have a mess of images. Sometimes the images are mixed up with others, so that they almost have no lines. Other times, they're so large and distorted, it's like they've come from dreams.

When Nathan walked back through the front door, still open from when he'd walked out, his bottom lip was trembling.

When I think of this day, it's not the knife I remember, held loosely by Nathan's side and then set down half-heartedly into the kitchen sink, pearls of bright red blood rolling along its blade. It's not the look of fear and wonder on Ella's small face as I grabbed her, ran into the house and locked her in the bathroom. It's not the feeling of jelly in my legs as I ran up the street, the thumping in my chest that felt like my own heart was punching me. It's not the horror of the blood, matted with fur, the loose pink tongue. It's not even the little turquoise bone-shaped metal tag on the leather collar – *Jasper* engraved in cursive – the moment I learnt his name. All these things I see, but the one that's up close, at the very front of my mind's eye, the one I see before I fall asleep at night, is Nathan's lip, his trembling bottom lip.

IF IT WASN'T THIS

Mary lay still for a few extra minutes as if playing possum with herself. Then she rolled to her side and lifted a hand to her face. Her arm felt heavy, and her hand as though it belonged to someone else. She brushed over the cold tip of her nose and circled her fingers once around each cheekbone, tentatively feeling up for her forehead. It was smooth and warm. Fine baby hair at her temples felt like spider webs. She swallowed hard, inhaled, and opened her eyes. Her breath fogged the air. It was just a dream, a stupid dream. She checked the clock. Six fifteen: she must have slept through the rooster and the milk delivery. It was the first day of winter.

On this same day last year she had discovered she was pregnant. So many anniversaries. They appeared before you, silently, like cats in the night.

She could hear Ron in the kitchen, the usual sounds. Mary and Ron had a rule about dreams. They were not to be shared. It was tedious to listen to someone recount a dream, even if that someone was either of them. Who cares about a dream? This was not to be confused with goals, a different type of dream altogether. These they shared. In Ron's study a small notebook with pencilled margins recorded their goals in his precise cursive handwriting that reminded Mary of a woman's. This might have bothered her, having a husband who wrote like a woman, but it didn't: she knew it was important that an optometrist have legible, accurate handwriting so people's scripts could be correctly made when they were posted down to the city. Their rule applied only to nocturnal, unconscious dreams, which meant Mary must keep last night's, and all the other ridiculous dreams she'd been having lately, to herself. She closed her eyes again and breathed slowly, feeling the synthetic fabric of her nightie chafe against the fold of flesh under her breasts.

It was one of a number of rules Ron and Mary had agreed upon during their six-month engagement. They would not drink alcohol, for example, nor would they ever let the sun go down on their anger. Theirs was to be a private marriage and already it brimmed with shorthands, acronyms and secret codes.

If she'd been chatting to someone new in town, Ron would turn to Mary and pose quietly, 'D?' and she would shake her head and purse her lips: 'Afraid not.' Meeting someone for the first time at bridge or tennis, Mary would lean across and whisper to Ron, 'I,' or 'D,' and sometimes, albeit rarely: 'ID.' An 'ID' would buoy them up, as if they'd found someone who spoke their language in a fast and foreign land. If Ron happened to see one of the Hastwells or the Murphys or the

Nitschkes, he'd finish telling Mary the news with, 'Ah, yes, she's an ID,' or 'Rich Hastwell, now there's an ID.' Decency and intelligence were attributes Ron and Mary valued highly.

They'd been married six years – not long in the scheme of things – but they were a formidable team. They were *The Hillmans*, and this was how Mary signed off Christmas cards before she folded them and slipped inside each one a copy of the 'Hillman News', conceived and typed each year by Ron.

Last year, as he'd handed her his final draft, he'd said, 'I didn't mention the baby, of course,' and she had nodded in agreement. She'd put down her secateurs, wiped her hands down her apron in an inverted V and sat down to read. Ron had written of their garden: the crop of cauliflowers, parsnips, beetroot and the prize-winning pumpkin. There were three paragraphs on the optometry business, the new doctor and second pharmacist, and the recent commitment to purchase their main street premises. He wrote of his golfing win back in March, the bridge tournaments, Mary's job at the chemist, and her success with floral arrangements at church for the growing number of weddings. How she may well even set up a floristry business down the track. She had taken the letter down to the post office and used the Xerox to make thirty-one copies.

If Mary had to cite the one key ingredient of their successful marriage, she would not hesitate to say 'communication'. Then she would add, 'You have to talk to each other,' and if Ron were there he would agree.

She wanted to tell Ron about the dream. It was different from the others. But then, maybe she didn't. Rules were there for a reason and, while this dream had troubled her, it was also nonsensical. She could at least see that. And saying things aloud could make them bigger than they were. Sometimes, one must keep one's own counsel.

In the dream Mary covered her face in oats, which she had mixed with water into a porridgy paste. Without knowing why she was doing it, she applied this mush in blobs around her nose, and on her temples and cheeks. Then she left the house, walked all the way down Hutchinson Street and into Gawler Street. She dropped in at the Institute and chatted to Meryl McKenzie, bought a loaf of sliced bread at the supermarket, and then stopped at the Optometry. There, she talked of octagonal fashion frames with Shirley, who sat behind the desk and eyed her with a furrowed brow. When she came home again and looked in the bathroom mirror, she was shocked by the full reality that she'd gone out in public with that stuff globbed on her face. She started clawing at it, dragging the muck into her hands, and it was then that she discovered there were remnants of fruit and vegetables also sticking to her face: slices of cucumber and bananas, and halves of plums, their mauve juice running down her chin and in between her fingers. At this point in the dream, she felt repulsed and confused. She felt humiliated. It was like a sick joke.

And now, awake and lying in bed, her fingers tugging the polyester rosebud bedspread up to her chin, she still felt those things: the emotions of the dream had accompanied her into consciousness. But it was a silly dream, it really was. She counselled herself not to dwell on it.

The nurse had told her she might feel 'a bit emotional' for a while. And she did, she had, but not in the way she'd imagined.

She'd imagined private tears but it wasn't like that. During the day she felt numb – she hadn't cried once. In her dreams at night she felt exposed and raw, like a skinned rabbit. Her dreams were filled with overripe fruit that were larger than life and oozing with juices. And there were knives; in her dreams sharp blades cut through a giant strawberry or a mountainous watermelon, the juxtaposing textures of steel against yielding fruit flesh sometimes waking her, making her shiver.

'Cup of tea?'

She nodded yes and listened again for the sounds of Ron heading back down to the kitchen.

This was their morning ritual. Ron would rise before her, dress, bar his tie, switch on the bathroom strip heater, collect the milk, let out the chickens and put away the evening meal dishes that he'd left washed and draining. Then, right before leaving for work, he would check to see if Mary was awake before he re-boiled the kettle for her cup of tea in bed. For as long as she could remember, Mary had never been good in the mornings. On her worst ones, when her brain resembled fuzzy wool dipped in thick molasses, she would inwardly weep with gratitude for this man who loved her and claimed her and brought her tea.

Something about his gait had changed in recent months. The sound of his shoes on the wooden floorboards was now slightly uneven, like a tilted metronome. It was the only thing that was different about him and it hadn't gone away. It was as if her miscarriage had dislocated his hips, somehow caused him a physical misalignment.

Stillbirth, not really miscarriage. She wondered what the

difference was. Her pregnancy had only been twenty-three weeks. Most people in town didn't even know. It was an unspoken competition: how far along you could be before people noticed. And then afterwards it was: how quickly you could look as though you'd never been pregnant at all. Lorraine Hastwell was the winner on both counts. Two weeks ago she'd given birth to a little girl they named Lorelie. After all the beautiful lorikeets, they said, though the Hastwells were hardly counter-cultural. Up and down Gawler Street Lorraine pushed the pram, her small hips in a tight-waisted skirt, her slender calves wrapped in long boots and her hair lapping at the curve of her back.

Stillbirth. Mary holds the word in the front of her mind where she can inspect the letters from a distance, as if she were merely their audience. Still. Birth. It was still birth, she thinks – she still gave birth – and that was the unexpected part. Like being in a car crash.

The baby was a boy. They'd wanted a boy first. Ron had even written it in the book: *Four children, boy first!* The exclamation mark a nod to their facetiousness, to the fact that gender was something they couldn't actually control. Unlike conception, which back then they had assumed was a given. Even so, like the other women in church, Mary had eaten all those bananas, just in case.

Ron had listed names, four of each, in order of preference: Mark, Michael, Greg, Phillip, Jane, Elizabeth, Carolyn, Tania. Never once had they imagined another possibility beyond a healthy boy or girl.

'Too little for a funeral,' the doctor at the Queen Victoria Hospital had told them. Dr Murphy, the new doctor at

Mount Barker hospital had sent Mary down to the city, where she didn't know anyone. It was hard to know if this made it better or worse. Better, she'd decided in the end. Her mother had posted her a white cotton handkerchief with a small rose embroidered in one corner in pale pink thread.

'This one just wasn't meant to be,' the doctor had said. 'You need to go home now and rest. And then you can try again. It's the best thing.' Then he patted her thigh as though he had something else to say but had forgotten what it was. There was a nurse in the room too, and she stayed after the doctor had left, smoothing the white waffle blankets and tightening the sheets under Mary's mattress. She was young, much younger than Mary. She couldn't have been more than twenty-one.

Mary could hear Ron clattering around in the kitchen, the kettle whistling on the stove. She smelt toast cooking. Or perhaps it was the Whitmores' wood oven cranking up next door. Soon enough, there'd be the sound of all those children waking up and singing out for this and that. Then the dog would start, and the goat the Whitmores kept for milk. Mary hated the earthy taste of the goat's milk and she had to swallow back on the memory every time a bleat carried over the wire fence.

Not long after the stillbirth, the nurse – her name was Olive – had finished tidying the night table next to Mary's bed and she had looked up, considered her. 'You know,' Olive said carefully, 'if it wasn't this, it'd be something else.' She had looked into Mary's eyes. 'Wouldn't it? You know what I mean, don't you?' Mary had been given a private room by then.

If there'd been others there, it might have sounded like

a cruel thing to say. But Mary had thought maybe she did know what Olive meant. There was always something wrong, something to be upset or angry or hurt about. Things were never perfect, and perhaps it could help to accept it. Even in small things, there would always be something not quite right.

They'd been 'trying' now for seven months. Such a strange code word for intercourse: 'trying'. Sometimes, when Mary saw a pregnant woman she would imagine her in the moment it actually happened: the moment of conception. Had the woman been completely naked? Or did she hike up her nightie like Mary sometimes did? Did the pregnant woman moan like they sometimes did in films? And then Mary would have to look away because it would suddenly feel shocking, and also demoralising to the woman, and to Mary for thinking of it. Everyone could see what a pregnant woman had been doing, and Mary didn't like that. Sometimes, she liked to imagine how she might arrange all this business if she were God.

Occasionally, she did enjoy intercourse with Ron, those times when it felt warming and cosy, like eating freshly baked bread with melted butter, or the satisfaction of turning out a cake when the whole thing stays intact, steam gently rising from its surface. Mostly it felt like another slightly uncomfortable but necessary job. It was important for Ron, though; she could see that. He enjoyed it, and that gave her different sorts of pleasure. She liked the power her body seemed to have over his – the way his face would contort into that helpless, pathetic smile that she didn't see at any other time. The way a mere glimpse of her naked breast would make him go hard. The way his eyes would narrow and the way, afterwards, he would say yes to anything. Yes to the new linoleum for the kitchen, yes to the twelve iceberg standard roses lining each side of the path to the front door, yes to this new bedspread.

Mary still hadn't adjusted to these cold winters, this being her sixth in Mount Barker. Lorraine Hastwell told her it was two degrees colder up here than it was in Adelaide, and it was probably even colder again than in Salisbury, where Mary had spent all the other winters of her life. She still found it strangely and vaguely surprising when the seasons came around again and again, as though the evidence she'd so far accrued to support the idea had not yet become conscious within her. She folded the bedspread back down to her lap and pulled herself up into a sitting position, propping both their pillows behind her. She'd wanted this bedspread the moment she saw it in the John Martin's mail order catalogue. She had wanted a baby too. She felt as though they were getting behind. Because they were getting behind; she didn't want to celebrate her next birthday. Her age was a fact neither of them wanted to say out loud.

Ron placed the cup and saucer on her bedside table, a thin rattle of china on china.

'There you go, love.' He leant in and kissed the top of her head. 'I'm off, then.'

'Ron?'

'Yes?'

'Nothing.'

He tilted his head toward her. 'What is it, my love?'

'Nothing, really. Have a good day. Lamb chops tonight. And I might drop in and help Shirley with the front window.

I've got some ideas for that. I'm only in the chemist over the lunch hours today.'

She remembered that the new Innoxa lipstick range would be in. It would be her job to arrange them all into their plastic compartments.

Ron stopped in the doorway and smiled at her a moment longer and then scrunched his mouth into a twist.

'I might see you later, then.'

'Yes. Off you go, then.'

Mary turned away from him and picked up her tea. She shuffled back a little and felt the scratch of the bedspread as it caught against her nightie. As usual, Ron had raised the holland blind so that she could see into the garden while she sipped her tea, and she focused on the small oak tree they'd planted right in the middle of the lawn. It was almost bare now; most of the leaves had turned orange and dropped to the ground. Ron had raked them clear and piled them into the compost. But a few remained on the tree, dark burgundy red now, curled and brittle at their edges. Maybe the tree refused to let them go, like a little old lady clutching at her purses. She counted them through the window, the warm teacup nestled across the dip of fabric in the space between her thighs. There were fourteen leaves left. She wondered how much rain and wind it would take to loosen each of those final fourteen leaves and strip them from the tree. Was it just a matter of time? Maybe they would all be gone by the end of this day. Then the tree would have to stand there alone, stark and bare, through the whole of winter.

ACKNOWLEDGEMENTS

My heart and deepest gratitude go to my first reader and most ardent supporter, David Washington. I can only hope I make him cry.

For making me laugh and inspiring me with her passion and understanding of the Arts, I thank Ruby Washington. For his constant challenge to make me think and question it all, I thank Amos Washington, to whom this book is dedicated.

I was deeply fortunate to be mentored in this project by Eva Hornung, who has taught me more than I can thank her for about writing, and life. I am also grateful for the encouragement and editorial wisdom of Susan Hosking, Nicholas Jose and Brian Castro at the University of Adelaide, where an earlier version of this book was part of a PhD in Creative Writing. Many people have shared insights and stories, offered encouragement, and read earlier drafts. I thank them all. For telling me about the Australasian Bittern, I thank Jolie Thomas. For their support of my writing and/or their keen editorial eyes, I thank Amanda Lohrey, Kirstie Innes-Will, Bronwyn Mehan, Linda Godfrey, Andy Kissane, Janine Mikosza, Patrick Allington, Pip Williams, Lynette Washington, Rachael Mead, Caroline Reid, Threasa Meads, Katherine Arguile, Sam Jozeps, Maurice A. Lee, Ele Williams, Heather Taylor Johnson, Amy Baillieu, Claire Bowman, Anna Solding, Sam Franzway and John Tague. For casting a medical eye, I thank Ian Mills.

I am blessed to have excellent and supportive family and friends, and I particularly thank Jan Baker and Tony Stimson for believing in this book well before it was finished. I am also grateful for the kindness of Jörg Strobel and Neryl McCallum.

These final pages were written in a small, Woolfian-inspired room, magically tucked at the base of a large ash tree, and for this I am indebted to Andrew Noble Safety Fifth and the gifted writer Rachael Mead.

For the publication of this book I thank the excellent people at Affirm Press – especially Martin Hughes, Keiran Rogers, Stephanie Bishop-Hall, Grace Breen, Ruby Ashby-Orr and Emily Ashenden – I will be forever grateful to have found such a brilliant publishing house. In particular, I thank my editor, Kate Goldsworthy, for reading and championing my manuscript with the sensitivity, insight and commitment that a writer can only hope for. To the excellent Jo Case: thank you for getting my book to the right people. And my thanks to the talented Karen Wallis for her cover design.

Writing this book was supported by an Australian Postgraduate Award, a Varuna Writers' House Fellowship and a CAL Cultural Fund grant, and I am extremely grateful for each of them.

I am honoured by the independent adventures many of the stories in this book have had: 'The Honesty Window' was first published in *Griffith Review* 55 (Brisbane, 2017); 'Something Special, Something Rare' appeared in *Best Australian Stories* (Black Inc., Melbourne, 2014), and was reprinted in *Something Special, Something Rare: Outstanding short stories by Australian women* (Black Inc., Melbourne, 2015); 'The Five Truths of Manhood' appeared in *Australian Book Review* (2013), was runner up in the 2013 *ABR* Elizabeth Jolley Short Story Prize, winner of the Readers' Choice Award for the same prize and shortlisted for the Fish Publishing Short Story Prize in Ireland; 'Raising Boys' appeared in *Southerly* (Sydney, 2013); 'Dancing On Your Bones' was shortlisted in the 2014 Carmel Bird Long Story Award and first published online in Spineless Wonders eSingles (2015); an earlier version of 'Jasper' was shortlisted in the 2010 *Wet Ink*/CAL Short Story Prize and first published as 'Barking Dogs' in *Wet Ink* (Adelaide, 2011); an earlier version of 'The Fourth Dimension' was first published as 'A Simple Matter of Aesthetics' in *Zettel Magazine* (Canada, 2014) and in *Breaking Beauty* (MidnightSun, Adelaide, 2014); 'If It Wasn't This' was shortlisted in the QUT postgraduate writing prize and appeared in *REX* (Brisbane, 2012); an earlier version of 'Here We Lie' was runner up in the *Wet Ink*/CAL 2012 Short Story Prize, a finalist in the *Glimmer Train* 2013 Fiction Open in the United States, and first published in *Short Story Journal* (The University of Texas at Brownsville, 2012); 'World Peace' appeared in *Influence and Confluence: East and West, A Global Anthology on the Short Story* (East China Normal University Press, 2016); 'May Twentieth' was shortlisted in the 2013 Alan Marshall Short Story Award and first published in the anthology *Unbraiding the Short Story* (U.S., 2014); and 'What I Wished' was awarded third prize in the 2014 Henry Handel Richardson Short Story Prize.